STAR STILL

CRYSTIANNIA RYCE

ISBN: 979-8-218-40130-6 (paperback)
ISBN: 979-8-218-48009-7 (ebook)
www.crystiannia.com

Cover Design by Fakel Barros of Stardust Book Services
Map Design by Joshua Hoskins of Stardust Book Services
Interior Art by Jonas Spokas of Stardust Book Services
Formatting by Rae Davennor of Stardust Book Services
www.stardustbookservices.com

First Edition 2024

*For those that want to be themselves,
but need extra time to shine.*

*For those that live in trauma,
and need a gentle escape to breathe.*

*Adventures don't need to be scary,
and love doesn't have to be uncertain.*

Mora Avi
Bay of Longhowl
Fi...
Mor...
Empire Of Calon
Unity Hall
Cartographer Joshua Hoskins
Stardustbook

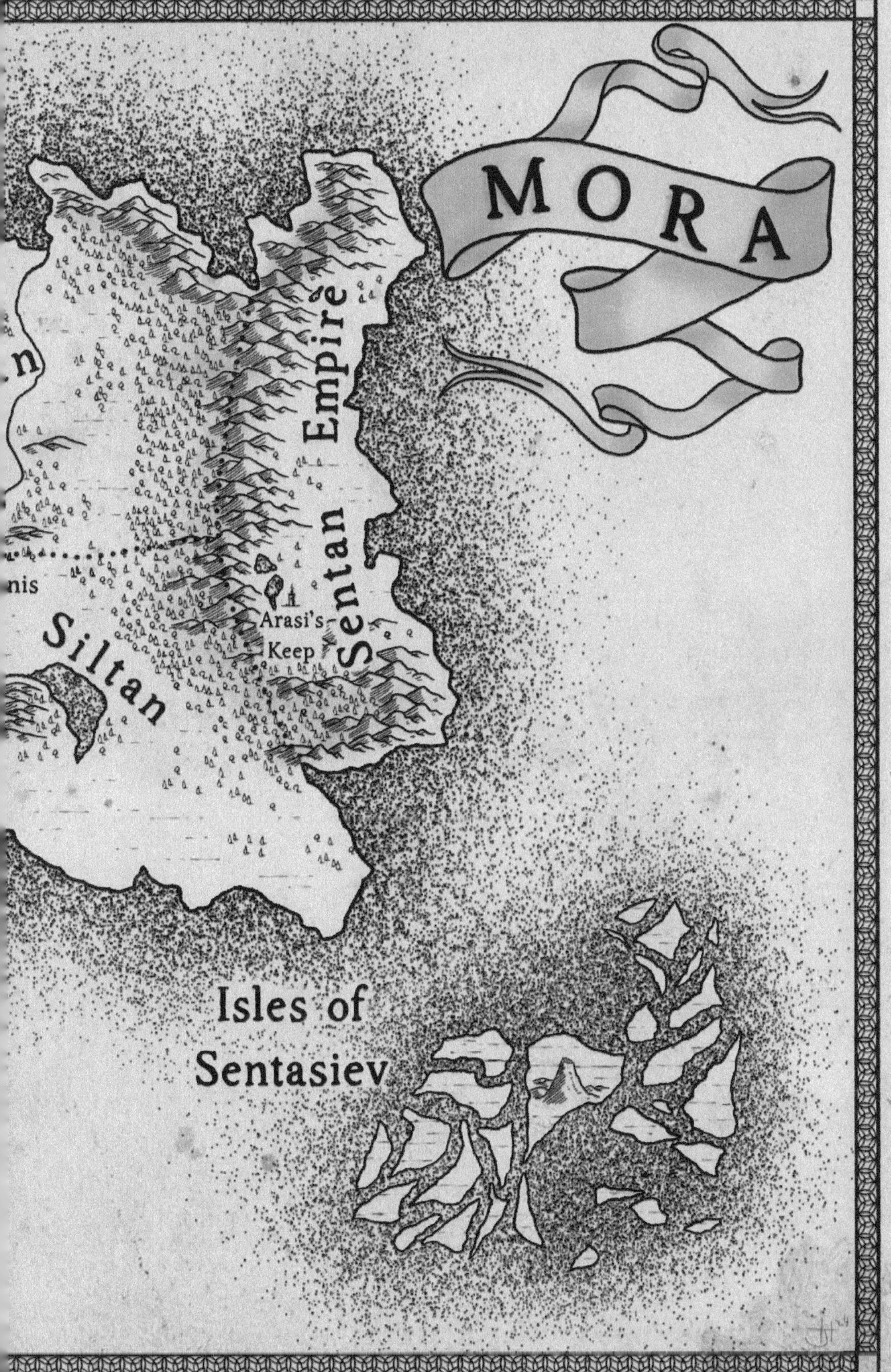

MORA
Sentan Empire
Empire
Arasi's Keep
Siltan
nis
Isles of
Sentasiev
Noctua Cartography

Chapter One

It was night, which everyone knows is the best time—just after twilight, when there are minimum people and maximum stars. The darkness did pose certain challenges, but nothing a bit of basic caster magic couldn't fix.

Rei thought he'd been careful to not draw attention as he carried an armful of quilts out to the field behind the keep he served in. Buried as he had been in managing his master's requests, he craved a few hours of uninterrupted peace. As he began merrily laying the ground cover, the faintest sounds of cautious footsteps disturbed the grass behind him. Approaching in politeness and not malice, a familiar presence as they came to a stop. He sat back on his heels and sighed, before turning to greet the young woman.

"What are you doing?" Kubo asked, wrinkling the quilt as she knelt next to him.

"Camping?" He assumed it was obvious.

"Outside?"

Rei stared at her, perplexed. "Is there another way?" He folded up one of the smaller blankets to use as a pillow and extinguished his lantern before stretching out. The half-moon cast just enough light to discern shadows, but not much else.

"Why, though?" She sat cross-legged next to him.

"Communing with the stars." It sounded more pleasant than telling her he wanted to be away from everyone for a little while. Rei would never be intentionally hurtful, and he could tell something was bothering his fellow caster.

"Oh. I thought you were out here to listen to the ground. Like me." She touched the grass just outside of the quilts. "It's been distressed."

"You mean the earthquakes."

Kubo nodded. "A result, I think, of the distress. The ground has an uneasy trembling, like a nervous opossum hiding under a log because she sees a woodsman nearby and her only desire is to fill her empty belly with the apple cores at his feet."

"That is… oddly specific." Rei propped himself up on his elbows. "Is something besides quakes and opossums bothering you?"

"I don't like being in our quarters when Urie isn't around." She sounded embarrassed by her confession. "I need the background noise of his teeth grinding or I can't fall asleep soundly." Kubo relied on routine; having her roommate away disrupted her, even if they often bickered.

"Again"—Rei grinned—"very specific."

Kubo was the youngest of the three druidic servants and, while not a child, she maintained a plentiful amount of immaturity intertwined with her high intelligence. Rei couldn't be sure that wasn't on purpose; a defense she'd learned and hadn't put down yet. She had been at the keep for just over two years, but often it seemed she had just arrived.

"Join me, then," he told her. "I'll watch the heavens while you listen to the earth."

Kubo smiled gratefully. She secured her cloak, despite the warm air, and settled in beside her friend. They lay in silence for less time than Rei had hoped.

"Master Arasi has been more reclusive than usual lately," Kubo noted.

The older caster shrugged. "He does that on occasion. A druidic habit and nothing to cause concern. Although once, about a decade ago, he locked himself in his study for a solid week. Urie and I found out later that it had been accidental. A poorly executed spell had removed the doorway from his side of the room. But how were we to know that? From our perspective, the doorway was clearly present and locked from the inside." He paused, then added. "Had it gone on longer, I'm sure we would have attempted to knock the door in. Or scale up to the window. We heard movement, so we weren't concerned. Of course, we later realized that the stirring about was a raccoon family in the storage room next to his, so really, we hadn't heard him at all."

"Why didn't you just use your magic to check on him? Or open the door?" Kubo stared thoughtfully into the darkness as Rei struggled to find an answer.

"We were enjoying the quiet." It was true, and sounded better than, "Your senior magic users didn't think of that."

Amusement flickered in Kubo's eyes but dimmed with her next breath. "It's something more, though. Master is worried, and that's very unlike him." She waved her hand gracefully in the darkness, and Rei felt the slightest prickling of magic in the air. A moment passed before a moth with wings like stained glass began to flutter around her fingertips. Kubo smiled sadly as she watched the insect dance for her. "Everything is worried." With an unhurried gentleness, she spread her fingers, and the moth flew off into the night.

Rei grimaced. She wasn't wrong. Earthquakes weren't uncommon, but in the last year alone there had been a substantial increase in the number of quakes the continent of Mora was experiencing, each growing in strength. It was no coincidence that members of the druidic council had gone missing after investigating them, vanished along with their caster adjuncts. Malicious or not, the events were suspicious, causing rumors and bickering among the countries within the land.

As they stared into the sky, a star creased the darkness above as it fell somewhere into their world. "Do stars ever get replaced?" Kubo asked.

"No, I don't believe so." Rei answered, though he wasn't convinced that was true.

"Then, what happens when the last one falls?"

Rei shot a worried glance at her. In more than forty years, he'd never once contemplated that question. It made his stomach lurch. He stared at the stars still shining above them and let his thoughts wander with them for a moment. "We make our own."

"You're more optimistic than I am," she acknowledged.

He wasn't. Rei was only more adept at deflecting harmful thoughts.

It was training he had acquired from the earliest age he could remember. "You're carrying a lot of heavy thoughts tonight. Do you need a hug or a head pat?" he offered.

Kubo thought for a moment. "Can I lie on your arm?"

"Of course." Rei welcomed her alongside him and added a soft head pat as a bonus.

Rei knew they could not stop the stars from falling, just as much as they could not stop the ground from shaking. No magic caster nor druid had that level of control over the elements of their world. There was no benefit in denying it and even less in worrying about it. The only viable option to avoid madness was acceptance. Kubo would grow to understand that in time.

"Perhaps I am wrong," Rei added. "Or, at least, I hope that I am."

"You're seldom wrong," Kubo assured him. "But how so?"

Rei reached down and took Kubo's hand. He pressed her fingers into her palm, leaving one to point the way, and raised it to the sky. He playfully moved it back and forth, drawing in the air, until Kubo giggled. When Rei finally stopped, Kubo's finger was directed toward the western horizon, at a distinct cluster of stars the Sentan people knew as the constellation "foxtail."

"For decades I have been tracing these patterns with my eyes. I would recognize them before I would my own reflection. Foxtail has guided many a Sentan home since our ancestors first looked skyward. Fourteen stars curving out then back in." Rei nudged Kubo's hand slightly left. "But what is this, then? A fifteenth star?"

Kubo counted, and Rei was correct; another star was shining. "The scholars missed one all this time?"

"No, they were correct when the first of them, druids no doubt, made note of the pattern. But that was centuries ago, wasn't it? At some point, a new star joined their ranks. It wasn't a replacement; the other stars remained. Instead, newborn, with its own place in the sky."

"So the last star never will fall, will it?"

"Even if it does, my previous answer remains: we make our own."

"I like those thoughts. They're helpful. But can I lower my hand now?" Rei couldn't tell if she was being serious as he pushed her arm down back to her side. "I think I'd like to stay out here with you tonight. Would you mind grinding your teeth a bit?"

Rei smiled. "Not a chance."

Chapter Two

"That quake early this morning was the strongest yet; even my horse faltered. I'm sure half of Sentan were thrown from their beds."

"I've been thrown from my bed many a time; it's nothing a little calendula balm won't soothe." Binder Arasi was barely paying attention to what the empirical messenger was mumbling as he read over the gold gilded note she had delivered.

"It's unnerving."

"What is?" he asked, searching around his study for the source of her concern.

"The quakes. Do you not feel them out here?"

Arasi shrugged and shook his head. "A rumble not louder than my empty stomach."

"I thought druids were supposed to be in tune with the elements?"

Avoiding the messenger's comment, Arasi looked down at the paper in his hand and gave a pleasant sigh. "Thank you for conveying our emperor's correspondence. No need to await a reply. It wouldn't arrive in time anyway."

Once she had left, he sat back down in his desk chair, with the cushions all worn through, and thumbed through the papers in front of him. His mind moved swiftly and meticulously in thought even as he appeared the very vision of tranquility.

Sentan druids absorbed their powers from one of the elements of nature and were often expected to have their appearance predictably stitched from whichever one had chosen them. Whether the nature of their powers lied with fauna, flora, or stardust itself, they often incorporated an air of it into themselves. In this sense, Binder Arasi, as was the title placed on druids, failed remarkably. He, and even the white marbled ruins of his keep, was immaculate and didn't live up to the stereotype of a disheveled, yet potent, genius. About the only category he almost fell into was madness, though that was for effect.

"Kubo," Arasi called to his novice-adjunct standing just outside his study. "Urie isn't back yet, so I need you to take a quick trip." The bright-eyed young woman nodded eagerly and, without a moment of hesitation, pulled out her journal and pencil. The youngest of his trio of chosen assistants, Kubo was the most eager to learn Arasi's druidic ways, and even basic chore requests were met with little complaint. "In the city, the core library, I need you to retrieve the books by Kita, Earl of Forests—should be three volumes. Also, stop at the market on the way back and gather some pastries and wine from the Giro District."

"Expecting guests or taking a respite?" Kubo asked.

"Why must it be either? And who are you to question my orders?" The lilt in her master's voice betrayed his mock irritation.

Not one to suffer intimidation tactics, Kubo lifted neither her eyes nor her pencil. "Master, I do need the details if I am to bring back the correct quality and quantity. And, if it's for your personal respite, strength as well for the wine."

"Oh, yes. Impressive forethought." Arasi thought for a moment. "We're having guests. Let's say a dozen of us, so several dozen pastries. Vary them. No preference on the vintner but at least three flavors. It's just to supplement what I already have on hand. I will trust your judgment on this." He gave her a nod, dismissing her.

Rushing out of the room, eager to accomplish such an urgent task, Kubo promptly bumped into senior-adjunct Rei. "Careful, lightning! Why such a rush?" Kubo just held up her journal and dashed down the hall. "Important mission?" Rei asked as he entered the room and handed Arasi the maps he'd requested earlier.

"Indeed." The druid's golden-hued eyes lit up. "I sent her to the library."

"Clever." Rei grinned.

"I am quite proud! The conservators haven't let me pledge out books since a certain incident two years ago; getting my hands on them once more will be simply lovely. Shocked I hadn't thought of that earlier."

Arasi took the maps from Rei and spread each out on the massive birch wood table, which had borne his workload for decades. He tapped his bare chin in thought as he stared down at each one. His druidic binding focus was restoration, which came with the benefit of a youthful appearance, though his years were advanced, and not having to maintain a frizzy beard. He had attempted the growth decades ago, but the results were barely a chin-full of long silken hairs that unsettled him.

Awkwardly large but brilliantly detailed, the maps gave an overview of the entire continent of Mora. The Sentan Empire was the farthermost east country on the continent, its closest neighbors set behind a dense and unwelcoming mountain range. Sentan was nearly an island, crescent shaped and bordered by water wherever mountains didn't take over the landscape. The map's spread didn't show the sovereign borders or cities, only the topography and the lay of the land.

Arasi, who had been the Druidic Advisor to the Sentan Empire approaching twenty-five years, sighed as he studied the maps. "Not exactly what I was hoping for, but a start, nonetheless. The books Kubo is retrieving should paint a much larger picture."

"Will you be explaining what you are looking for to the rest of us, or is this purely for personal amusement?" his eldest apprentice quipped.

"My own amusement, of course!" Arasi pursed his lips and pointed to the jagged ridges drawn along their country's western border. "Have you never grasped how voluptuous and carnal these peaks are? So reminiscent of certain anatomical bits. Who wouldn't allot their time to poring over these flat, mildew-scented sheets of parchment?" The druid was able to keep his tone serious, but the mischievous glint in his eyes gave him away. "Details to come after I have them shared with the appropriate parties first."

"Do you require anything further, my sage?" Rei respectfully teased, as his master set out transcribing supplies for a later task.

"Sage?" Arasi balked. "Where did that come from?"

"Would you prefer 'Old One'? If you're starting to confuse a flaccid, I mean, flat, sheet of paper for a wom—"

"Mind your manners, servant!" Arasi threw up his hand to silence him with a glare of mock indignation. "Besides, you aren't terribly younger than me, and I look better." The druid gave an impish wink and beckoned Rei to walk alongside him. "Flaccid? Really? You went with flaccid?"

He shrugged. "First word that matched flat."

Rei had been an adjunct, a trusted assistant with learned magic capabilities, for almost half of the druid's empirical tenure, and their relationship had long surpassed the borders of master and apprentice. Arasi had remained his first and only master, having arrived at the Academy the day before Rei was to begin his first official post as a caster. In the market for a new apprentice, Arasi selected Rei as his adept-adjunct, bypassing novice. Arasi had never bothered to review the other graduates and not once regretted his choice. In the years they had worked together, they had become more than apprentice and master; Rei had become a brother to him.

Highly skilled, Rei had achieved top ordinations in two areas of the Lyceum Paths, the Sentan Empire's official university. Few graduates achieved such honor. Three paths of study were offered at the school: Lyceum Path Fortitude for magic users, Lyceum Path Regiment for military service, and Lyceum Path Curative for those who sought medicinal training. The empirical druids, magic users born with the enhanced ability to bind the will of their environments, often sought apprentices from the graduates. Rei had bypassed the entrance exams and had his choice of paths. He had excelled in each class he was assigned.

The two made their way down the short vestibule to the common hall. "We're having visitors; I may have forgotten to mention." Arasi rarely forgot things, and so Rei anticipated the remark was added for his amusement. "Foresight tells me they will be arriving soon. Before sunset, at the latest. Further assistance is not required here, so I'll ask you to kindly oversee the guest preparations and instruct the servants. Guest rooms, expand on dinner, the usual lavish accommodations."

"Lavish?" Rei stopped and cocked his head.

Arasi turned and pursed his lips. "Well, yes. Lavish for our humble home." He locked eyes with Rei, his mischievousness apparent. "Emperor Ki-tae will be gracing us in a day or two, and I'd like to put on a more regal air."

"Then, who, may I ask, is arriving this evening?"

"Oh," the druid added, in mock afterthought, "we're also expecting our dear friend from Calon, Prime Mediator Cadence and her standard travel guards." Arasi delightedly watched as Rei's expression lit up. "Attend to anything else you think would be appropriate."

"Of course." Rei bowed his head, turning to leave before the words were even out of his mouth. His exit had been swift, though not as outwardly eager as Kubo's had been. Standing suddenly alone in the hall, Arasi couldn't help chuckling out loud to himself.

Since the Mora Unity Pact had gone into effect several years prior, the Prime Mediator of Calon, Cadence Allis, had been a routine visitor to Arasi's keep. The role of Prime Mediator, the continental representative of Calon sovereignty, was to be Calon's eyes and ears across the continent, addressing needs or potential threats.

The Sentan Empire, as it now stood, was roughly 600 miles east of the Empire of Calon, which made up the western border of Mora, with smaller countries nestled between them. The continent had learned decades ago, when an unanticipated enemy surrounded their coasts, that banding together was in everyone's best interest, and the Unity Pact sealed that belief. A crack in one country's defenses would lead to a crack in another's and so on.

With their home continent of Mora experiencing vast geographical disruptions in recent months, they were meeting more frequently, hoping to discern the cause. While the reason for Cadence's visits was to conduct official business, it didn't stop the old friends from enjoying their time together.

Prime Mediator Cadence had made the trip to the eastern coast dozens of times. Though the roads of Mora were tailored to merchants, making them easy to traverse in most parts, the travel time was long with stretches of peaceful forest solitude. Sentan was a less rigid environment than her home of Calon, and Cadence looked forward to being back in that atmosphere each visit. She loved Calon, for the diversity of both its people and landscapes, but the hustle and constant propriety wore at her. One of the reasons she had chosen the position of Prime Mediator was the allowance to travel and live life away from Calon's heaviness. The role also provided a reason to visit Binder Arasi, who she counted among her closest friends and most amusing collaborator of trouble.

Cadence and a modest troop of Calon guards came within sight of Binder Arasi's keep slightly before dusk, as the druid had glimpsed from his gift of foresight. Relief washed over her, and she gave her horse a gentle nudge to speed up when she detected a shock of dark purple among the noticeably still green forest leaves. "You don't blend well." She grinned as she came up on Rei, who was patiently waiting on the side of the road.

"Neither do you," he countered. Cadence dismounted, and they bowed their heads slightly in formal greeting. "Welcome back to our home." They shared a friendly, quick embrace.

"I'm happy to make my return. My apologies we weren't announced sooner, but I'm sure Arasi knew we would be here today."

"Arasi saw as much, so no apologies needed." He offered to take the reins of her horse as they walked up the path toward the stables, the Calon guards close behind. Rei gazed up at the treetops as they began to walk, attempting to shield the grin on his face.

From the moment Cadence and Rei had been introduced, it was plain to Arasi the two had won each other's attention. However, to the druid's frustration, neither would budge. Occasionally, Arasi would give Rei subtle nudges, but his modest adjunct would shrug them off. More than occasionally, he would give Cadence blatant nudges, but she followed suit. It led to a stalemate that Arasi had to fight back the urge to progress; their affections weren't his trial no matter how much he enjoyed being the spectator.

"I hope you weren't waiting long. We would have found our way from here on our own."

Rei waved off her words. "Not at all. It was easy to sense your arrival. As well as the fact that you're still our guests, and it would be rude to leave you on your own. Besides, it was pleasurable to get outside for a bit and enjoy the view."

"What view?" Cadence laughed, looking around at the forest surrounding them. "The trees you see every day?"

"Mmm, yes. Exactly those things." Rei gave a tight-lipped grin that Cadence pretended not to notice. "Living on the grounds of a restoration druid's home gives everything the impression of eternal spring, even when I can see autumn just over the hills. It gives you an appreciation for each little change."

As the stable hands took the horses from the guards, Cadence unstrapped a large bundle and handed it to Rei. "The western maps your master has requested." Her smile turned to a grimace. "Can you please be sure he treats them with care and force him to return them please? I'm well aware of his history with books from libraries across the continent and our allies across the northern seas as well. These may not be books, but we do need them back."

"I'll watch over them intently—you have my promise." Rei grinned, bundling them into his arms. "My master has been unusually enamored with maps as of late. He'll be excited, to say the least." Cadence noted the tone in his voice and could tell she had missed out on something humorous.

Cadence motioned for her guards to follow as she and Rei stepped onto the narrow stone footpath up to the keep. "It's been almost half a year since you were here last, hasn't it?" Rei noted. "Have you been well?"

"For the most part. Tired, a bit distracted with everything going on. Usual Calon politics and social duties, but those will all resolve someday."

"One of these decades," Rei half joked.

"So it seems these days. I'll be thankful, though, when life returns to some semblance of normal and we can perhaps focus on less dire situations?" She threw a sidelong glance at the handsome caster. Rei had been Arasi's second in command for a decade. Cadence had only met him herself a few years ago, but he had grown to be one of the people she most anticipated spending time with on her trips. "How have you been?"

"Eh, we've been good, I suppose," Rei responded. "Arasi has had Master Urie and I running rampant, gathering a litany of spells, both archaic and modern. I'm certain our errands pertain to the quakes Mora keeps enduring. Nevertheless, ssh"—he smiled—"we don't want him to know how much we know. He's been trying to keep it secretive so no one panics. Which ends up causing more panic. Judging by his attitude and late hours, he is giving the impression he's onto something. It hasn't given us much time for our other work, but priorities, right?"

"Priorities," Cadence agreed, "but I have a feeling you're about to get all of your questions answered in the next few days." She reached up and tugged gently on a lock of his hair. "Your hair has gotten long, and your purple seems especially bright. I like it. You're looking well, at least. Are you?"

"The benefit of working for a restoration druid." He grinned. "Keeps you looking well beyond your years. Sometimes I even struggle to remember Kubo isn't a child. I swear being around Arasi ages her backward."

"All good, but I did mean how are *you*, specifically." She shot him a coy smile, and Rei quickly turned his face away in an effort to conceal the blush permeating his tawny cheeks.

"Oh. Well, how I've been isn't all that important compared to everything else. Fine? I guess? Haven't killed Kubo and haven't let Urie kill Kubo. Or Kubo kill Urie. So I've stayed on top of my work." Speaking with Cadence always took Rei a few moments to adjust to; it made him both elated and nervous.

"Kubo's sweet, but I can see where she'd grate on the nerves a bit. Arasi's last letter mentioned you taking her under your wing, much like a true teacher. He said he thinks her skills are far more advanced than even she realizes. She needs guidance, and Urie definitely doesn't have the same patience you do. How he is such an exceptional father is a mystery. The girls must use up all his patience when he is with them. You, on the other hand, always possess an overabundance of patience," she complimented. "Kubo's training must take up the bulk of your time, though."

"I grew up with a highly energetic younger sister. Kubo isn't much different than she was at four," Rei joked. "So it hasn't been too troublesome. Her presence has even made me a bit nostalgic. Don't tell her, though. Our plan is to make her think we are ready to throw her into the oubliette as soon as Arasi's back is turned."

"Arasi has an oubliette?"

"No. At least not yet. Kubo doesn't need to be aware of that."

"Are you sure Urie hasn't secretly created one?"

"Um. No. No, I am not." They both giggled, realizing it wouldn't be entirely out of character for their lovable, but petulant, friend.

Arasi's keep, a centuries old remainder of a once-grand castle, came into view through the brush and trees. It was always a welcome sight, and Cadence instantly felt at home. She poked Rei's shoulder. "Still doesn't answer how you have been though. Not everyone else. You."

"I'm always good. You know that," Rei replied cheerfully, looking up at the stars just starting to make their presence.

"I do know that. Very suspect, if you ask me."

Rei furrowed his brow. "Suspect? Should I be insulted?"

"No, I'm only teasing."

"I can tell." He smiled. "Rest assured, as of this moment, I am quite good. Sincerely." Rei stole a covert glance at her, reminding himself of just why he felt that way.

"Good. You still owe me a rematch at pachi, and I've been practicing. So I'm sure your mood will be less elated after."

"Is that so?" Rei scratched his chin, contemplating her words. "I admire your confidence."

"Thank you."

"As misplaced as it is in this case. You can't practice pachi; you're either skilled at the game or you're not. I've only let you win in the past because you were a guest."

Cadence shook her head and laughed. "Oh? For such a wonderful human you can be surprisingly dreadful."

Chapter Three

Binder Arasi greeted Prime Mediator Cadence and her guards warmly once they reached the entrance hall of the druid's home. "My beloved Mistress of Calon! You've returned to me!" he gleefully exclaimed as they embraced tightly. "Oh careful, love. My ribs aren't as solid as Rei's," he chided in her ear as she pushed him back.

"Always happy to return." She smiled, and her words were sincere. "Shame it's been nothing but seriousness, lately." Cadence turned and bowed to the tall figure next to the druid. "Captain Devi, always a pleasure to see you. I am honored you came out to greet us."

Captain Devi bowed in return. "Of course! It is always a delight when you return. Spending all day surrounded by these word warriors gets a bit stale. Now I get to chat up someone with more practical experience," she said, smiling like a giddy child. Captain Devi had been the head of Arasi's personal guard and his protection for as far back as Cadence could recall. The captain's traditional military bearing made for a striking counterpart to the slender druid and his casters.

Arasi nodded. "I was trying to simplify another announcement, and this group proves difficult to gather. We will have a very special visitor joining us in a few days," he said, enunciating the word special.

"The emperor?" Captain Devi caught his eye and smirked.

"Oh. Completely obvious?" Binder Arasi appeared genuinely perplexed.

"A bit," Captain Devi agreed.

"Ah. Well, correct. Our beloved Sentan Emperor, Ki-tae Kara-Shon, will be joining us. We have critical matters to discuss, and as the palace is under renovations, we will meet here." Arasi beckoned them down the hall. "He will have an inconspicuous escort with him, so no grandiose entrance this time. We anticipate no concerns, but we still need to fortify the protection spells here, and in the surrounding forests. Since Urie still hasn't returned, Rei, you and I will begin at first light. Captain Devi, kindly follow empirical protocols as per the usual."

"When is the emperor's expected arrival?" Captain Devi asked.

"Assume two days."

"So soon? My lord, we talked about short notice before—"

"I know, I know"—Arasi held up his hands—"but this is not on me. Our emperor either altered his agenda or wasn't forthcoming on his actual plans, and my foresight doesn't work well on him. Between safety and brashness, he has his reasons. And I do adore him for it!" Arasi grinned and threw his arm around Cadence's waist. "You're tired, but let's take a short walk along the garden before dinner to stretch and catch up. Rei and Captain Devi, please take care of the guards and meals, and so on."

"'Renovations?'" Cadence teased as they began to walk.

"Of sorts," was all Arasi would respond with.

Emperor Ki-tae Kara-Shon, or Ki-tae to those close to him, had been the ruler of Sentan for three decades and was as well-loved for his cunning and benevolence as he was his gaiety. Ki-tae had been the first of the royal bloodline to be born on the continent of Mora and not their homeland of Sentasiev, the Isle of Sentan. While still a brash youth, he had captained armies to victory and, when the fighting came to an end, embraced the peaceful life. He and his beloved Empress Le-ni led their people to fruitfulness, easily sealing his place in the hearts of the Sentan citizens, particularly that of Binder Arasi.

The emperor had been to the druid's estate on many occasions, both official and casual. Binder Arasi was his preeminent advisor, and the two had a close relationship, which did not go overlooked. That Cadence, the voice of Calon across the continent, was also here meant this small gathering had larger intent.

Walking along the garden pathway in the dimming light, Arasi invited Cadence to select the flowers for the centerpiece of the emperor's arrival. The violets and gladiolas she gathered didn't surprise him. "As always, you favor the purple beauties."

"The peonies are red," she pointed out. "Purple and red are regal colors, aren't they? What's more fitting for your emperor? Besides, you don't have any lilies or orchids in your garden. Those are my favorite." His garden was a gift of Mora's constant mild weather, but the mountainous grounds of his keep weren't favorable to all varieties.

"My emperor has plenty of orchids in his own garden." Arasi adored watching Cadence bloom when she came to visit. Any sliver of peace he could give her brought him joy. "Calon's stability is ebbing, isn't it?" he asked.

"Nothing travels faster than news of misfortune. We were one of the last bastions, sitting so far from all of the action. Until now, the quakes had been contained along our north-western border, with little damage to the towns. They're starting to reach farther in, and while there's been no damage, Emperor Jiyan is well-aware how that may change without warning." She bent to cut another peony, tenderly stroking the petals as she placed it in with the others.

"Have you been well, love?" Arasi's words were uncharacteristically soft.

"As well as any of us have been." Cadence gave an approving nod as she inspected the flowers. "Our world has been difficult lately. That trickles down into all of our lives. We're surviving, though."

"Mmm, true. We all have full plates." The druid added further gladiolas to the bouquet. "How is your plate?"

Cadence shook her head and pushed the flowers into Arasi's arms. "At the moment, empty. And I am starving." She turned back toward the keep. "Certainly, dinner must be ready."

*
**

Concluding a generous dinner of tasty foods and enjoyable conversation, Cadence joined Arasi in his private sitting room. Changed into the same robes the casters wore, she reclined on the couch and, at his insistence, was drinking a glass of wine while he readied for bed. "This tastes horrible." She grimaced at the first sip. "Should it be this tart or was it opened too soon?"

"That's only because your tongue prefers ale. Like any respectable military whelp," he chided from behind his dressing screen.

"I'm not a military whelp!"

"Were one or more of your caretakers military? Were you trained at a military academy? Did you serve on missions in cold, rainy, hot, and/or dry lands? Have you killed anyone in a fight and not been charged with a crime?"

"You're aware those apply to almost anyone born in Calon, and you are well aware my parents were not even remotely trained in anything that would callous their fragile hands. So, no, not quite a whelp." She smiled and put down the glass with not much more than a sip touched. "When was the last time you met with Emperor Ki-tae?" Her smile hinted at something unsaid; secrets were few between the two of them.

Arasi pursed his lips as he emerged and thought for a moment. "I can't say for certain. All of us have been so preoccupied lately. I'm glad for his visit, though." He poured a glass of wine for himself and joined her on the couch. He wrinkled his nose and stared at the glass. "A little tart, otherwise you haven't the slightest what you're talking about." Arasi gave a forlorn sigh. "Pity this is strictly empire matters."

"I'm sure that won't put a complete damper on your happiness." Cadence patted his arm. She knew the strong emotions the druid held for his emperor were deeper than just loyalty and respect. "It will be good to finally sit with Ki-tae and not be stationed on a diplomatic concourse surrounded by pomp and circumstance."

"Or by obscured roles?" Arasi raised an eyebrow.

"Obscured how? My role as Prime Mediator puts me in the room, not at the table. It is our dear Calon Emperor's role to be our voice, and maintaining that is critical to my temperament and all-around emotional health, thank you."

Arasi shrugged. "Obscured. But indeed, this will be fun for you! Ki-tae has a way of making you feel you're the only object of his attention, even if a dozen others are pulling at his sleeves."

"The consummate politician."

"Absolutely," he agreed. "Ki-tae was born into it. Being a leader is all he has ever known, and he plays the part exquisitely. He lives for it. You'll be terribly smitten with him, though you likely won't think him as handsome as Rei." Arasi sipped his wine, half hiding his smirk. When Cadence didn't respond, he turned toward her and smiled. Despite her age, she was youthful and lovely as ever, more so in the soft shade of pink her face was turning at his comment. It was easy for Arasi to read her without using his druidic influence. He stared, waiting for a response, but was aware she wouldn't acknowledge anything he said on the subject.

"Rei has been a wonderful colleague." She grinned. "Why you insist anything more exists is beyond my head. Every time I visit, you make these wild assumptions."

"'Colleague,'" Arasi chided. "Interesting you didn't say 'friend,' almost as if you want to put distance where there is none." Cadence gave him a long stare and shrugged. "Aside from that pretty rose-petal coloring crossing your cheeks at the mention of his name, I've been watching the both of you, and it's obvious what your thoughts are. Frankly, it is disgusting to be put through this over the last few years. Teasing and batting of lashes, sidelong glances, teaming up to torment those around you. Why not pass secret notes next? Ugh."

Cadence threw back her head and let out an exasperated sigh. "You make us sound like children. We are long past that age."

"Exactly! No need for the false innocence; you're both decades into adulthood with all the glorious experience that comes with age. So bed him already!"

"Arasi, I've not traveled hundreds of miles across the continent to bed one of your assistants."

"Don't tell me you haven't thought about precisely that. I've seen how you bite your lip when you're standing behind him."

Cadence held up her finger to his lips. "Don't. You best mind your words, love." She was more abashed than angry.

Arasi took her hand from his mouth and suavely kissed her fingertips. "You should be flattered—Rei is far more than an assistant, you realize. An excellent match, if you ask me."

"Arasi, I do so love you, but…" Cadence trailed off, uncertain what to say. "Relationships in our positions, well, we know how those often go, and you are keenly aware my situation with the council doesn't permit it. I live my life as the Calon Empire dictates, and involving others makes it complicated. Add to it physically and culturally miles apart. It doesn't breed happiness in the long run."

"I remember a time when you would be fine with just the breeding part and ignore the long run." Cadence choked on her breath at his comment and smacked his shoulder.

"Play offended, but everything I have spoken is true," Arasi said through laughter. "I remember those nights in coastal taverns; you would hunt your prey, I would hunt mine. Compare quality over breakfast. Over lunch, if the hunt went exceptionally well! Sometimes swap. Such fun times!" He crossed his arms and peered at her with an air of naughty nostalgia. "Neither of you are chaste nor bashful as you both pretend. You could show up at his door tonight and I wouldn't see either of you for days!" He paused, taking a drink. "The hesitation is because you want more than mere pleasures with him. I don't blame you. You're older now. You're scared."

"Older? Scared? I'm starting to have doubts about both this friendship and your sanity." Cadence rubbed her forehead in exasperation. "Does Rei know you talk like this about him?"

"Oh, for certain. Doesn't care and unquestionably does not listen. Rei is like you: willfully blind and full of excuses to deny his own happiness."

"And what of your happiness, dear one? Obsessed with your work for ages now, living for the occasional royal visit or clandestine trip to the palace? Are you happy?"

"Just because my relationships are more focused and less public these days, doesn't mean I am not happy. Once all this, whatever this is, gets resolved, you might just be seeing a lot less of me for the very reason of my happiness."

Cadence winced. "Bit rude."

"Well, ideally, I'd rather you be seeing less of me and more of someone else. We're both overdue."

"Deserved for you and Ki-tae, but not in my plans, Arasi." Cadence picked up her glass and recoiled as she emptied the unpleasant contents before turning the glass upside down on the table next to them.

Arasi's words were true; Cadence had fallen for Rei almost immediately. Pinpointing what it was about him that captured her was no simple task—his jovial nature and the fact that he was lovely to look at with his always-sparkling amber eyes and wild hair were certainly a starting point, but each moment with him increased her desires. In truth, it made her just as sad as it did happy. "Besides, I've seen ladies far younger and more supple than me line the fences waiting to catch his eye. I doubt he is as lonely as you imagine." A trace of melancholy was tucked in her voice. "Rei has his pick."

"Interesting." Arasi raised an eyebrow. "Because from my view, they seem awfully disappointed when he passes by without a glance. Not surprising, considering most of them are young enough to be his daughter or little sister, at best. Rei's always busy, even when it's not work I've given him. Studying, training, riding—he has a full agenda. There was a time when he would at least attend the Eventide Market every month, but he hasn't been to one of those in, oh I'd say, over a year. Or perhaps three? Might possibly be more. Oddly enough, that staying in seems to coincide with meeting someone. I just can't remember precisely who that was?" He looked accusingly at Cadence, and she balked.

"Certainly not my doing."

"Not directly." Arasi shook his head. "I wish I had introduced you sooner."

"I don't know if it's the travel, the wine, or you, but I have a headache." Cadence ran her fingers through her tangled tresses and made a face. It had been a long trek on dusty roads, and she cringed as the dirt in her hair gathered under her nails. "I need to wash up. Then I'm going to bed."

"Alone?"

"Yes," she curtly responded, and kissed the druid's cheek as she pushed up from the couch.

"You remember where Rei's room is, right?" Arasi teased as he walked her to the door.

"Good night, dear heart!" Cadence called over her shoulder as she disappeared down the hall.

Chapter Four

It was early the next morning, as the sun was lighting orange paths through the forests surrounding the keep, that Binder Arasi and Rei hurriedly walked the perimeter, reinforcing the existing wardings for the emperor's visit. Mora hadn't seen conflict in years, but they knew to still be careful. A visiting monarch was as much an easy target for criminals as for assassins. It was midmorning when they completed their task and were coming upon the main pathway when Urie, Arasi's junior-adjunct, saw them.

"Back already?" Arasi asked. "The trip must not have been as deadly as I'd thought." Urie was Arasi's favorite to tease. The man was a skilled learner and talented caster, but too often cynical, which Arasi hoped to counter one day. Where Rei was older but optimistic, Urie was younger and pessimistic, which made watching the two interact quite amusing. Kubo was still trying to find her place in the mix, which was even more amusing to witness.

Urie nodded. "Yes, not dead. Apparently." He hooked his thumb toward the clearing near the back of the keep. "Are either of you aware of what appears to be a fight of sorts going on? Doesn't sound dangerous, but Captain Devi is shouting more than usual for her." Arasi and Rei exchanged confused glances as they headed in the direction of the ruckus.

Between the stables and what would have been the former castle's parade ground, they found a sparring circle had formed. "What's this?" Arasi asked. "Are we enemies now?"

"Ah, just fun." Captain Devi grinned. "Training with a bit of…" She glanced at Cadence.

"Um… monetary incentive?" Cadence shrugged.

"Incentive, huh?" Arasi replied. "Odd way to say 'betting,' isn't it?" He grimaced at the winded guards leaning against the fence posts or sprawled on the grass. "I gather we are not doing well, are we?"

"Not at all. Our guards haven't gotten out much." Devi winced as one of her guards took a solid hit despite the cushioned staff the Calon guard was using. "They're getting stagnant. I told you we need more training missions, but you want to fix everything with a—" she waved her hand to mimic casting.

Captain Devi had served as Arasi's head of guards the longest of any prior captain and firmly believed in muscle over magic. Druidic guards often had a caster or two in their ranks but as a whole consisted of military trained personnel or graduates from Lyceum Path Regiment. She preferred graduates fresh from Regiment training, before they could be swooped up and made hard-nosed by assignments in other areas, such as Principal. Unfortunately, that also meant they weren't the most elite or disciplined. But they were moldable.

More excited about the scenario than their master, Rei and Urie pulled water and apples from a supply bin and moved closer to the action. The casters settled onto the grass for an up-close view. "We haven't had such exciting entertainment in ages!" Urie grinned.

Rei agreed. "Even though our side is going to keep getting pummeled. Captain Devi's guards aren't well trained for melee weapons, like those batons. Probably better grapplers if it were true hand to hand."

"I'm not sure what those words mean other than our side appears to be at a disadvantage."

"Precisely what those words mean. So if you want to drop a few coins, pick the other side."

Arasi winced as he observed two of the Calon soldiers get knocked down by one of Captain Devi's hefty guards, who then simultaneously lost his balance and fell on top of them. Cadence and Devi were barking directions and cheering their guards on with glee. Despite the outcome of the matches and bruised egos, the high-spirited camaraderie and excitement was a welcome change of pace from the usual quiet of the grounds. It was a nice bit of life for a change.

"Not getting a chance to fight much," Cadence pointed out to Arasi, "isn't necessarily a bad thing. With the prevalence of magic users in Sentan, physical combat isn't a great necessity. In an actual fight, one of your casters could simply bind an opponent. Elsewhere on Mora isn't so lucky."

"Depends on the situation, doesn't it?" Arasi scoffed. "Personally, I'd rather keep it that way, though they should at least be capable of fending off adversaries without losing their breaths in the first few moments." A grin slowly began to light up his face. "But these are personal guards and not held to the continued Sentan military training standards."

"Maybe they should be." Captain Devi shrugged. "As I have routinely suggested." She had only pushed for that standard the last decade.

"We should arrange a demonstration among two more worthy opponents. Your best fighter versus mine. Show the novices how it is done," Arasi suggested to Cadence.

"Your guards are already not faring well," Cadence gloated, "and Captain Devi is out of fresh fighters."

"Not Captain Devi's best fighter. *My* best fighter."

"Casters versus guards? That is hardly fair. You'll launch flames at us or something of that ilk," Cadence protested, uncertain her friend was being serious about the match. She turned her head toward Captain Devi, who was visibly amused by the idea.

As the last of the beaten guards stumbled to recoup in the grass, Arasi stepped over to the fighting pit. Cadence and Captain Devi exchanged confused glances as they followed him, stopping beside where Urie and Rei sat. "No magic. Strictly physical combat. Equal as can be." Arasi smiled.

Cadence leaned down and swiped a piece of the bread Rei was eating. "I don't see how a caster has the same ability to defeat a trained fighter without using their natural born cheats," she challenged, poking at her friend. She was aware her statement was defective, but it garnered the desired facial expression from Arasi. "However, pick someone, and I'll personally have a try. It's been a few years, but I'm less rusty than any of your challengers."

"Personally? Are you sure? You tease about my guards, but you haven't been tested in combat in a decade! Although the consequences if you get hurt…" The druid's eyes were twinkling as he let his words trail off. Cadence ignored him and jerked her head toward the pit. "Excellent, then! Fight Rei."

"What?" both Cadence and Rei said in unison.

Rei peered up at the commotion behind him and stood. "I'm fighting now? Who exactly?"

"Your master has lost his mind," Cadence informed him.

"You're fighting Cadence." The druid was beaming in his smugness.

Cadence turned from Arasi to Rei, then back to Arasi. "No. I like Rei. I don't want to hurt him. He's not much bigger than me—I think I even outweigh him!"

Rei was both pleased and offended by her remarks.

"Don't be silly. He's got almost two inches on you. One, at least. Besides, he's mostly muscle, and you've gotten mushy in the last few years"—Arasi poked at Cadence's arm, grinning—"and squishy. Rei, exercise restraint, please. Your challenger is still our guest."

Cadence gave Arasi a withering glare showing she'd rather take the baton to *his* nose but sighed and relented.

"How did I get roped into this?" Rei demanded. He glanced down at Urie for support, but his friend looked even more excited about the match than Arasi.

Captain Devi patted Rei's shoulder and gave him a gentle shove toward the pit. "Binder Arasi picked you as his best fighter. I haven't seen you scrap in years, but I'm well aware of your expertise." She winked.

"Cadence has been on her feet all morning, so if you target low, we should be quick to win."

Rei mulled over the advice for a few seconds but shook his head when he felt Cadence's eyes on him. He gave Arasi a final glare of protest but dutifully stepped forward into the cleared pit. He knew full well what Arasi was playing at, but he had to admit, he kind of liked the idea.

"Rei? Really, Arasi?" Cadence bemoaned as she ducked under the wooden fence around the sparring area. "He may be your best caster, but I'm not sure the result will be in your favor." It was doubtless that her old friend had other reasons for initiating the bout, and she planned to make the druid pay for his wickedness later. Cadence walked toward the center and faced Rei. "You're aware that we are both being taken advantage of. Arasi is making us his puppets. We don't have to do this."

"Might be fun. One drop and we're done, master is pleased with his stunt." Rei paused before adding, "Kindly accept my apology now for your defeat, dear friend." He bowed dramatically.

"You approve of this? Fine, then. I won't spare you just because you are not ugly and"—she studied him up and down—"wispy." Space cleared around the two as they were handed blunted sparring batons.

"'Wispy?'" Is that what she actually thought? Wispy? What began as little more than a civil dance began to morph into something more tense as the competitive nature of the two became piqued, and Rei kept hearing the word "wispy" replay in his mind. He was lean, not wispy.

Cadence was impressed to find Rei was able to match her blow for blow and moved with greater finesse than she'd given him credit for. She assumed he would be a decent challenge but anticipated having to pull her blows against the caster. Her politeness dissipated, and she did not hold back, now obviously enjoying the task at hand. Rei had little trouble countering, though a finishing blow was still out of reach.

Much to the crowd's amusement, they had been sparring for longer than any previous match. "I applaud that this is taking more time than I anticipated. At least someone has been maintaining discipline." Cadence swiped low, but the waster she was swinging proved too cumbersome to hit its mark behind his knee.

"Wait! 'Taking more time'?" Rei stepped back and held up his hands to her. "We can stop; give the word. You're undeniably drained, and I have actual work to do," he taunted, trying to force an opening. Cadence knew the ploy but let him carry on. "You're winded. I'm bored. I'll announce I'm conceding so you can maintain your self-respect in front of your guards and sneak away to take a nap." Holding the baton behind him, Rei tilted forward on his toes and grinned.

"You're a bit more muffin-like than I expected," she responded. "I don't want you getting hurt if I decide to take this match in earnest. I would be wracked with remorse if you skinned your knee. So, if you would like to quit, as a spell-less caster is inclined to do, you won't be at fault, and Calon will accept our win."

Rei readied his baton once more. "Apologies, my comment was too abrupt, and I've reconsidered. Sentan will not give a concession. Instead, I'm offering you an opportunity to rest your weary bones, and *you* may concede."

"Casters certainly are a waffling sort." She swung at him before her sentence finished.

Turning away from the volley of blows, Rei spun and connected hard with her thigh. Even he internally winced. "At least with casting, you need to stay on your toes—you never know what will come your way. With physical combat under controlled conditions, there are only so many things you need to anticipate. It gets predictable. Like your last round of attacks." Rei grinned.

Cadence clenched her jaw. Whether it was from being tired or in fight mode, she couldn't tell, but the grin that she'd grown to adore suddenly pricked her skin. Atoning for her 'predictable' blows, Cadence drew her fist back and immediately regretted that action as she watched Rei fall to the ground.

"I'm sorry," she apologized, reaching a hand down to him without thinking. Instead of accepting her offer, Rei swept her legs from her and pinned her shoulders easily to the ground. "Ow!"

"Finally!" Devi shouted as Arasi and Urie applauded along with their guards. "I told you to focus low!" Even the Calon company applauded their win. The bout had unarguably been the best match of the day and a solid ending to the training.

"Unfair!" Cadence snapped from beneath Rei. "He cheated!" Cadence stared up at Rei in shock.

"I cheated? How? *You* punched *me*," he reminded her.

"I…well, yes. Was that unpredictable enough for you?" They both laughed.

"You can get off her now," Binder Arasi called over his shoulder as he began to walk back to the keep, smiling to himself.

Rei glared over at Arasi, and if Cadence had heard him, she didn't acknowledge it. "I knew I could get to you, but I was expecting you to swing with the baton, not your fist." He smiled down at her, in no hurry to concede his position, and Cadence made no effort to push him from her. With a hint of hesitation, Rei stood and offered his hand. "Hard punch, though. I expected you'd have solid combat technique."

"Well, you were quite unexpected." She brushed herself off and accepted his help. "Where did you learn to fight like that? You're better than Captain Devi's guards."

He shrugged. "I have varied skills."

Cadence dismissed her guards for lunch and followed Rei back to the keep. "And where did you learn such varied skills?"

"Training. Studying. Life lessons. You have a false expectation that casters are only focused on one skill set. We're not all wiggling fingers and incantations. The Lyceum Academy doesn't send casters, or anyone, down one path with blinders on."

"I don't think that." She paused for a moment. "No, wait, you're intentionally being misleading." Cadence stopped and grabbed Rei's arm. "You're redirecting me again. I'm asking about you, and you are telling me about casters. Why?"

Rei moved to disagree but stopped himself. "Habit," he responded, and shrugged again. "I'm starving. If I hadn't been out doing the wards all morning I would have overtaken you in short order." She could hear the delight in his voice as they began walking again. "It was less embarrassing for you this way."

"Well, if we hadn't an audience perhaps I would have let you overtake me." She smiled and jogged past him. After a moment of clarity, Rei stopped and watched as she disappeared down the path, his face burning, but not where her fist had landed.

Chapter Five

Binder Arasi's keep was nestled at the base of the mountains on Sentan's western border. The humble village, a short walk from the druid's home, was sparsely populated, but the merchants always had more interesting goods to offer than the largest ports in Calon. Vendors in the town were forbidden from calling out to passersby and instead took to putting chimes in front of their shops to draw attention to their wares, which Cadence adored. Each shop used their own variety of chimes, and it gave the streets an ethereal resonance. She relished the soft notes over barking shop keeps and wished other merchant districts would instill something similar in their shops.

There was also a well-kept local secret that Cadence was eager to visit as evening fell. Making her way past the shops, she followed a worn dirt path leading up to the base of the mountains. The hot springs located along the town's eastern border were spacious and the respite of many an aching body. At this time of the evening, the spring would have the least amount of visitors, and she was in need of a satisfying, quiet soak.

It had been years since Cadence had put that much abuse on her body, and her arms and backside stung, as well as her knuckles where she'd made contact with Rei's jaw. She felt terrible about the hit for several seconds before he landed her on her ass. Cadence had trained for years with the Calon military, completing her commission as division leader; that a Sentan caster was able to knock her down, although it hadn't been quick, was a surprise. As evenly as they appeared to be matched, Cadence didn't put it past Arasi that maybe Rei had been enchanted. Or, more likely, not been forthcoming about some hidden talents.

The steam from the torch-lit pools filled the air with a musky fragrance, and Cadence took a deep breath. Hot springs this large were not common in Calon, so she treasured these visits. She undressed in one of the small changing huts and carefully tread into the water, the heat pleasantly prickling her skin. She had been correct that the spring wouldn't be crowded and was pleased when she found a walled-off nook to settle in. Cadence pushed back against the wall and was watching her toes float to the surface when she heard a familiar voice nearby. To her far left, a shock of purple hair appeared over one of the short privacy walls dividing the spring. Smirking, she silently swam up behind him, resting her arms against the barrier.

"How's your jaw?" Cadence startled him.

Rei grinned as he realized it was her and turned toward the wall, cognizant to stay below the waterline. "How's your backside?" he retorted, concentrating on maintaining eye contact. The steam and orange-flamed torches around the hot springs didn't allow for much visibility, but Rei wasn't taking any chances that his eyes would rudely wander.

"I've had worse," Cadence informed the caster. She hadn't thought the logistics of this conversation through and hoped he didn't spy her gaze drifting. She'd only seen him in his gray and blue robes, the standard caster uniform, which were fine. Rei's current outfit, or lack thereof, was much better at showing off his lean, muscular frame. She was both appreciative and disappointed about the stone wall between them. Cadence kept her focus on his eyes, which she realized didn't make her any less distracted with how the torchlight illuminated them to the color of honey. "I am still sorry for the punch. Mostly."

Rei touched his hand to his chin. "Thankfully, I don't bruise easily."

As he raised his arm, Cadence caught sight of black markings against the tan skin of his inner bicep; she recognized them on sight. Swiftly stretching across the wall, she grabbed his wrist, extending his arm toward her and allowing a clear view. Realizing what caught her attention, Rei guiltily looked away as she studied the symbols etched onto his skin. Cadence glared up at him accusingly. "Principal Regiment?" As Prime Mediator, Cadence was required to recognize the insignia of all the units on Mora. Principal Regiment was the elite unit of the Sentan military trained at the Lyceum Academy; any who made it through at least one mission were permanently marked with the unit's name.

Rei clenched his jaw and averted his eyes, trying to hide his smirk. "Funny story…"

Cadence jabbed her nail into the markings and glared.

"Ow! What?"

"Talk about cheating!"

"Cheating? How? I believe you're the one who went against the rules and punched me, so…" Rei shrugged.

Cadence's usual amiable face grew stern. "You are a druid-adjunct—since when do regiments become casters?" She was more curious than angry. A sharp divide between the two areas of study had always existed, and the two almost never convened. Even the casters who were trained as guards, such as some of Captain Devi's units, weren't from Regiment. If you became Principal Regiment, the upper echelon of service, you died as Principal Regiment.

"Arasi, and you, took advantage of my lack of information. No wonder he was so quick to nominate you to fight. I thought he was just being…" Cadence stopped, and her gaze softened from anger to disappointment. "That's a dirty trick and absolutely cheating on his and your part."

"Don't be cross, please." Rei felt his heart falter in shame, though he was also thoroughly amused. "Please, Cadence?"

"Not entirely cross, just surprised and disappointed. All these years, you never share anything when I ask and then use that lack of intelligence against me." The letdown in her eyes devastated Rei. Cadence moved back and sunk down into the water, her black hair fanning out around her.

Rei leaned over the wall. "Hey." The beads of water on her pink skin shimmered in the dim light, and Rei fought to remind himself to keep his focus ahead, not down. "Cadence?"

Cadence closed her eyes and ignored him until Rei splashed at her. She was torn between being irked and wanting the details. "What, liar?"

"Ouch. It isn't a lie if you didn't ask. You failed to do your research." He regretted his words the moment they left his lips, and he mentally bemoaned the lack of a spell to erase them.

She glared for a moment. "I did." Cadence closed her eyes and remained calm.

"Afterwards," Rei said helplessly. He wasn't helping himself, and yet, something about the discussion was amusing to him.

"I often ask, and you never elaborate on anything or talk about your life. Honestly, I could have asked 'What did you study?', and your response would have been 'books' or 'lessons.'" She cocked her head and waited for his response. "Am I wrong?" Rei shook his head as she glided back over to the wall. "So, then. How does a soldier become a druidic apprentice?"

Rei kept his voice low. "I was a born caster, with high natural abilities from a young age. I was adept and bored, so dreadfully bored, before studies even began. I was feisty, so…"

"Because of the hair?"

He ignored her. "… and I loved the physical element of Regiment training. The strategizing, the planning. The combat." Momentarily, he paused, wanting to give her as honest an answer as he could. "It made me think better of myself to be a defender instead of someone who could just put on tricks. So I chose that path for myself instead and excelled. Thus, landing my place with Principal Regiment."

"Still doesn't explain why you're back to being a caster and with Arasi. If Regiment was your desired calling, and what you completed at Lyceum, why not remain on that path? Most die as Regiment. Why the change?"

Rei shrugged. "What we desire is not always what we get." He took a breath and continued, "I was clumsy, overzealous, and let slip my caster abilities in a way I wasn't able to hide and don't want to relive. The councils for all three paths became involved. The whole situation was a mess. When they were done lecturing me, they laid a new path for me, and that's when Arasi stepped in. His offer was more intriguing than theirs. So here I am."

"Interesting how much you've omitted in that to appease my question at the most basic level." Her tone was icy, but Rei picked up on the hurt within.

"Binder Arasi does not want every detail shared. I did answer your question, though." He splashed at her again, attempting to lighten the mood once more.

"Without a doubt, you are hiding a great deal more to your story," Cadence accused, but Rei only smiled and shrugged. "All these years." She shook her head. "I'm disappointed in the both of you. Scam artists." Cadence splashed him back with a smirk and swam off. So much about him she still didn't know and longed to, but that would have to wait until another time. When she was less angry.

Rei stared longingly after her as he sunk down into the hot water to clear his mind. It didn't work.

Moments later, the caster was still lost in pleasant thought when something jarred him back to reality. Rei looked around the nearly vacant spring, but nothing seemed amiss. He was one of the few bathers left as the night closed in and everything was calm. Listening to his instincts despite the peacefulness, he climbed out and began to dress. Rei had just pulled his boots on when he felt a slight rumbling beneath him and turned to see ripples forming in the water.

With no time to alert anyone to help, Rei immediately put up a barrier around the springs and yelled at the remaining bathers to get out of the water and away from the mountainsides. Seconds after the last toe left the water, a loud crack rattled the area as a boulder cascaded down into the barrier Rei had put up. Without thinking, he reinforced it as a barrage of smaller ones came down around the springs.

"Rei?!" He heard Cadence's voice calling out and turned to see her rushing up behind him.

"I shielded the area around the mountains," he told her, but the townspeople—"

The sound of the barrier cracking under a slab of mountainside cut him off. Rei and Cadence grabbed one another and escaped into a changing hut as jagged chunks soared toward them, followed by several feet of fast-moving water that had been displaced.

The hut bore the brunt of the damage, but the deluge of water took the supports out from under it. Rei was still focused on maintaining the barrier as Cadence caught sight of the thin roof above them splitting. She grabbed onto Rei with one hand as she pulled the remains of a bench over them with her other. She hoped it would provide at least some protection as the rest of the structure collapsed around them.

Long minutes passed before the air around them became eerily quiet. Splintered bits of the former hut clung to their wet bodies as they stared breathless as the water quickly receded.

"Thank you." Rei grimaced at her before a stark realization jolted through him. "The town!" Rei jumped up and helped Cadence to her feet.

"Kubo was taking care of them," Cadence informed him as they hastened through the mud and rocks. "I met up with her as I was returning to the keep. She said the atmosphere was too tight, then suddenly the ground quivered. She ran through, ushering everyone inside and putting up barriers as I came to get you to help. But you were already on top of that."

"Somewhat," he said disappointedly. "I wasn't expecting the mountains to start raining down on us." Rei peered up at the village road lanterns still swaying above them; half of their lights were extinguished. He pulled a branch from a passing tree and twisted the end until it glowed as a flameless torch. He passed it to Cadence and made another for himself. "Careful," he warned, "it's not fire, but it can still burn you."

"What is it, then?" She waved the light in front of them; the path to town was unhindered, just sodden from the waters.

"Magic?" Rei shrugged.

"Well, thanks for unraveling that mystery," she replied. Cadence peered ahead as the structures from the town came into view. The village light posts were still standing and brightly lit.

Rei exhaled loudly. "Everything seems intact." The relief washed over him stronger than the waters had. They made their way into the heart of the small town and found Kubo, sitting exhausted on a garden wall. "Are you dead?" Rei asked her. Cadence glared at him.

"I can't breathe, but judging from my aching head, still alive," the younger caster responded without opening her eyes.

"You did excellent," Cadence praised. She sat down beside her, and Kubo put her head onto her shoulder.

"I did do great." Kubo sighed sleepily.

Letting Kubo and Cadence recuperate, Rei performed a hasty

inspection of the town alongside several town officials who'd come running out into the fray. The shields that Kubo had put up worked remarkably well at keeping the rocks and boulders from doing any harm. Tipped over water vessels and cracked windows seemed to be the extent of the damage away from the springs. As Rei was speaking with the officials, a breathless Urie and Captain Devi came riding up to them, followed by members of Arasi's and the Calon's guards.

"We could hear the earth splitting from up at the keep. What did you break?" Urie questioned his caster friend.

"Not me. Not this time," Rei told him. "The quake didn't seem bad, but it triggered an avalanche."

Captain Devi dismounted. "Casualties?"

"Doesn't seem so," one of the officials said. "We're lucky that he and the young one were here to help."

Urie's face dropped. "Kubo. Is she okay?"

"Fine. Just exhausted. Cadence is keeping an eye on her. You and Captain Devi should survey the springs. The damage is the worst there, and I'm certain that everyone was able to get to safety. But just to be sure, please."

"Of course," Captain Devi replied, ordering the guards to follow her.

"Arasi directed me to spend the night here. In case of aftershocks and such," Urie informed them as they walked over to where Kubo and Cadence were sitting. "The two of you look rough." He frowned. "Do you need any help walking back? I can give you my horse."

"I think we'll be fine." Rei thanked him and turned to the others. "Ready?"

"Make Rei carry me back to the keep," Kubo groaned. Cadence looked up at him, and Rei smiled in agreement.

"The damage may well have been far worse," Cadence stated as they made their way back to the keep. "He can only do so much, but I'm sure Arasi has everything shielded as a precaution just the same."

"He does," Rei grunted under the weight of the caster in his arms. "Part of the warding put up this morning was also a barrier and extends as far into the town as we can manage. It doesn't stop the quaking, but it's effective against the resulting shifts. Lightens the load. Speaking of which"—he groaned—"I think Kubo is getting heavier with each step."

Chapter Six

Emperor Ki-tae Kara-Shon of the Sentan Empire was the epitome of grace and intelligence, with all the flirtatiousness of a novice rogue. It was a fitting demeanor and certainly made diplomatic confrontations involving him more fun. He entered the keep with a flourish of black and deep-crimson robes, flashing his infamous smile, and immediately embraced his most trusted advisor before enthusiastically greeting the others. After the pleasantries were finished, Binder Arasi escorted the emperor and Cadence to his private study as dinner was prepared.

While Cadence was privy to the clandestine relationship between the two, it was obvious to everyone that he and Arasi were besotted with one another and did little to hide it. Cadence had once asked how the empress felt about the flirtations and whispers, to which Arasi had stated, "She and her husband have their own rules about marriage, as divine as they are." He left it at that.

Arasi presented his emperor to Cadence with a deep bow. "Up close, you're lovelier than Arasi let on." He grinned, his Sentan accent more marked than Arasi's. He took her hand and kissed it, shoulder-length blonde waves, touched with emerald green, falling against her skin.

"I would say the same for you, most cherished emperor." Cadence batted her lashes and flirted back in a way Arasi had never seen, catching the druid off guard. "I was well aware you had such a devilish smile, but I didn't expect your eyes would be so divine."

Ki-tae grinned widely, his dark eyes lighting up. "Such flattery! No wonder the Calon council makes me keep my distance from you! Which one of you will I choose for company tonight?" he teased.

"At one time, both." Arasi smirked and wrapped an arm around Cadence's waist. Cadence shook her head and sighed as Ki-tae's grin widened. It wasn't untrue. "She is too smitten with my proxy now, though." He winked, letting her go.

Ki-tae mock pouted. "Pity. An excellent choice, though! You've chosen your proxy well."

"Proxy?" Cadence raised her eyebrow and stared at the druid. "Proxy as in?"

"Scion?" Arasi shrugged, but Cadence understood what he meant. "He's come a long way from hostile soldier to eager caster."

The emperor made himself comfortable and beckoned Arasi and Cadence to sit on either side of him. "Eventually, up and on, then." He smiled. "The changing of the guard should be interesting."

"Should he accept," Arasi said, bringing some wine and glasses over to the couch for them. He looked at Cadence and held a finger to his smirking lips, indicating this conversation wasn't for Rei's ears. The druid poured some wine for each and sat back. "He's passed everything that I've thrown at him, even dealing with our overeager and heavy-handed novices without a single gripe. He holds back though, completely unwilling to fully open up, which impedes his druidic journey the most. Rei has plenty of potential to unlock, and his binder talent to assess, but possibly not much time to do so."

Cadence knew from past conversations with Arasi that he had early hopes for Rei to take up the druidic path. Only a small fraction of casters had the gift to do so, and he believed with Rei's skills it would be a natural progression. Unfortunately, Rei didn't share the druid's belief and his mind hadn't appeared to have changed. That did nothing to dissuade Arasi from still planning for it.

They sat for a few more moments in leisure, enjoying the wine before beginning the real reason for his visit: what was occurring in the middle of the continent to cause the crops and vegetation to start dying and the lands to be under a constant barrage of tremors. Like the other countries, they had thought it plague or drought, but after reviewing the maps and tracking the course, Arasi realized it was something far worse; he just needed confirmation before they rattled the other nations with the news that something impactful was looming.

"How impactful?" Cadence asked.

"Terrifyingly, depending on where you happen to be standing," he told her. "What you felt last night, magnified an infinite amount. An enormous landscape divide is coming. Whether it disrupts part of the continent or all of our surroundings is what we need to figure out."

"This has happened before," Ki-tae reminded them. "It's a natural occurrence that we've experienced firsthand. Our native continent changed enough to rid us from it." The reason the Sentan people came to Mora originally had been to escape the destruction of their homeland.

"True, but this hints at being different somehow," Arasi added. "Almost as though something else is causing the occurrence. I'm not saying what is happening is unnatural, but the cause of these occurrences appears to be. We don't want to cause panic by announcing this, though. We need to be cautious."

Cadence understood. The mountainous regions of her home were so recognized for shifting that their experts had written several texts on the subject, but it was always predictable in pattern. "How do you intend to figure this out?"

"We can't, though we have started researching," the emperor explained. "What we can do is understand the risks and try to plan for the safety of everyone if Calon can get the other countries to understand the urgency." He sighed. "Many still view Sentan as an outsider when the news is not pleasant."

"The maps I was reviewing gave some very obvious clues as to what we might be dealing with," Arasi told them. "Kana Kimin is a region not far from here known for an underground molten river. When our envoys first arrived, they noted the changing landscape in that area. The once larger castle that this keep is a remnant of is even mentioned in their discovery journals. Quite an interesting read."

"Oh! Yes!" Ki-tae piped up, his eyes brightening. "The Monti Annals.

It is an interesting volume, as far as scholarly texts go." He grinned and leaned into Cadence. "The essays entail what our people experienced before they made it over the mountain borders. The book includes a whole chapter about the envoys all too close to succumbing to cannibalism until they came upon a herd of what they thought were wild pigs." He laughed. "They weren't pigs but were still mostly edible. Then another chapter on the more impish pastimes they took to during the winter months when they were stuck indoors and then had to account for the boom in mouths to feed!"

"I'm not remotely surprised you're fond of that chapter." Cadence smiled and shook her head.

"Well, those of us who paid attention to the rest of the book found the other chapters a bit more useful." Arasi brought the conversation back to its critical roots. "The Monti Hills are only a solid day's ride from here. The Ona family controls most of the open lands in Satura and are quite knowledgeable about the area, as they've been there from the first generations. They not only have maps that go back ages but also the most up to date documentation as well. Cadence, mind going to gather some details? I'd like you to be able to act as the eyes of Calon with this and gather what detail you think is vital to bring back to your emperor and council."

Emperor Ki-tae voiced his agreement. "Seeing what is happening through another's eyes is the perspective we need to be sure we aren't missing anything. We want to be able to explain what is happening as best as possible. Everyone needs to understand, even those that haven't experienced the worst of it."

Cadence nodded. "Of course. That is my purpose, isn't it?"

"Thank you," Ki-tae bowed his head gratefully. "Lightheartedness aside, we do need to move rapidly in order to understand what is happening to our world and it seems that only Calon and Sentan have the resources to do so these days. For some reason, our countries are the ones being spared the level of destruction the others are encountering." His tone turned a bit solemn. "Empress Le-ni has already ordered the stockpiling of supplies and clearing of buildings to be used as shelter for our people should that need arise. We are hoping it doesn't become a necessity, but just in case, we want to be prepared. Naturally, our protections extend to those outside our borders."

"We are one continent. We will do whatever we can to keep our people protected, whether the lands are safe or not." Cadence stood up. "I'll speak with my guards and inform them we'll be traveling in the morning." She turned to Arasi. "Please let me know who will be guiding us and have them meet us at the stables first thing."

"As it happens, I do have someone intimately familiar with the area and the family you'll need to speak with. They'll make sure everything is taken care of." Arasi went to the door and called in Kubo, who had been stationed in her usual position outside the door. The druid wrote a note for her to deliver to Rei, which she did so quicker than necessary.

*
**

The young apprentice was breathless when she reached the adjunct's study at the other end of the keep, worrying Rei and Urie, who'd been inside going over spells.

"We're not under attack—you have no need to sprout wings every time Arasi asks you to do something," Urie groaned. "It makes us think something is wrong."

"The enthusiasm is appreciated," Rei added. "Just tone it down a bit. It leads Urie to believe work is expected of him."

Kubo apologized and handed Rei the note.

"All well?" Urie asked.

Kubo nudged Urie. "He's unhappy," she observed.

"No." Rei sighed. "I'm not. Arasi needs me to take a small trip tomorrow. I mean"—Rei shrugged—"I'm not happy, but I'm not unhappy about it." His face didn't look very convincing.

"To where?" Kubo asked.

"My hometown." Rei let out a long breath.

"Isn't that a good thing?" Kubo asked, confused.

"Eh," Urie muttered, "I hate mine. No one back home liked me. Except my parents."

"Yes, but that's because you're as serious as salt." Kubo smiled.

Urie balked, offended, but Rei shook his head. "That's not nice. At least salt adds flavor. Life would be bland without salt."

"Thank you, Rei."

"Of course, too much salt makes you thirsty and can kill you, so it's a balance," he added, smiling.

"See?" Kubo nodded. "That's why everybody likes you, Rei. You're a perfect balance."

"Right?" Rei jokingly held his head up. "Thank you, Kubo. Well, not everyone appreciates that about me. For instance, in my hometown." He then took a pencil and turned the note from Arasi over, writing one of his own. "I'll need you to take this to Cadence, please."

"Perhaps you should deliver the note in person?" Urie smirked, batting Kubo's hand away from the outstretched paper. The older adjunct gave him a sideways glare and shook his head, keeping the paper thrust toward Kubo, who looked unsure as to whether she should listen to Rei or wait for Urie to continue. "Most everyone likes you, Rei. Cadence, most noticeably." Urie pulled the paper from Rei's hand and, after a short stare-off, sighed and passed the paper to Kubo.

"Oh!" Kubo suddenly gasped, and Rei glared at her and then Urie. "Likes. Oh! Likes! Do you? Does she? I mean… How do you know?"

"I know these things. That's how I got a wife!" Urie looked smug at that.

"Because you know things!" Kubo grinned.

"No. Because, unlike someone else, I opened my mouth and said something." Urie stared back at Rei, who put his head down in his hands.

"You are both terribly amusing. Well, terribly something." Rei groaned into his palms. He loved his adjunct family, but this was not a conversation he wanted to be a part of, let alone the subject of.

Urie sat down on the desk and tapped Rei on the head. "What is the issue here? You were damn near engaged to Asande, so you are familiar with the correct protocols for these affairs. I realize that was a few years ago, but you still can't be thinking of her?"

Rei grimaced and shook his head. "Of course not."

"Cadence is kinder than her," Kubo offered. "And prettier."

"Funnier," Urie added. "Smarter too."

"True! Maybe you shouldn't say anything, then." Kubo chuckled.

"Great. Perfect. Thanks, friends." Rei sighed. "This isn't as easy for me. Lessons learned and all that." Urie sensed that Rei was uncomfortable and put his hand on Kubo's shoulder, shushing any further comments.

"I'll take the note to Cadence," Kubo told them. "Should I take another for Arasi?"

"No." Rei waved his hand. "I'm sure our beloved master will have filled her in on the details. These are only the travel plans since we will be accompanying her."

"Arasi and Cadence have a very close relationship." Kubo smiled.

"They've been friends a long time," Rei told her.

"I know they had assignments together. I'm guessing assassination attempts and all that. Extraordinarily secretive business." Kubo's eyes lit up. "Intriguing, but neither of them will say exactly what it was. Any idea what the missions were?"

"Uh…" Urie paused, uncomfortable for a short moment, and then smirked at Rei. He could read his friend's thoughts trying to discern whether or not to scar their young, somewhat naive friend.

"You aren't quite ready for that information," Rei explained, stifling a laugh, as Urie nodded in agreement.

Kubo shook her head and left with the note.

"I am not prying into the details of why you and Asande fell apart." Urie turned to Rei once they were alone. "But enough time has passed that it shouldn't hold you back anymore."

"It doesn't. But—"

"But what? It is obvious Cadence is quite fond of you and has been for some time. She tolerates you more than Lia did me when we were first courting. Sure, Calon and Sentan have a long distance between them, but if things begin to grow, well, you have options to consider, halfway points. All the way points?"

"You're bothering me," Rei said coldly.

"You are bothering you," Urie retorted, hopping from the desk. "I'm not going to say anything more after this, but listen to me. Brother, let Cadence know. That is all. Simpler than the spells in our first-year books."

"I didn't study first-year spells, or any spells," Rei reminded him. "I was in Regiment training."

"That explains so much."

"Meaning?" Rei glared as he saw the rude comment forming behind his friend's eyes.

"Meaning, goodnight." Urie clasped Rei's shoulder and wished him sweet dreams.

His thoughts still lingering on his conversation with Urie, Rei made his way to his master's quarters.

"We need to speak with the Ona family about the soil their gardens are made with," Arasi explained when Rei arrived at his door.

The Ona family's wine, from the Satura province, was the most renowned in the Sentan Empire. In recent years, it had become in demand outside of Sentan. The method the family used to grow the plums and grapes made for an unbeatable delicacy that had gained appreciation throughout Mora.

"They bring it in from the floor of a mine in the Monti Hills, and it looks like that's where the quakes are originating. It is not anything they are doing, but I think they will be able to give us insight." He turned to

Rei, who was looking more bothered than usual. "It also may mean that they are near one of the devastation spots once things begin to spiral. I don't like putting undue pressure on you, but you understand why you are the best choice to get this information."

Rei met his eyes and nodded. "I understand, and I have no qualms, though I don't understand why Cadence must come with."

"We need someone, other than from Sentan, for credibility," the emperor explained. "Sometimes people need to see a situation through the eyes of their own kind to believe."

Arasi tapped his fingers along the rim of his wine glass, staring at the deep-golden liquid inside. "If your hesitation for the Prime Mediator's company has to do with familial concerns, that is for you to come to terms with." The druid raised his eyes and was met with the slightest of scowls from his assistant.

"Oh?" Emperor Ki-tae raised an eyebrow and glanced from Arasi to Rei, eagerly awaiting the details.

Arasi moved to speak, but Rei beat him to the words before they left his mouth. "I'm certain that Binder Arasi has mentioned my family is from Satura. My sister is the matron of the Satura family, overseeing the vineyard with her husband."

"Oh indeed. Is this a conflict, then?"

"Not at all," Arasi piped up. "My dear apprentice is given to over-thinking. His sister will adore Cadence, unquestionably welcome her into the family." He didn't even attempt to conceal his smirk.

"Excellent, then. You best get prepared so you can leave together at first light," the emperor said, dismissing Rei.

Rei's head was pounding as he left the room. He had no doubt his sister would be overjoyed to see them and delighted to meet Cadence. Her reaction wasn't what worried him.

Chapter Seven

At the first blush of morning coloring the sky, Cadence and her company set out, following Rei on the daylong trek back toward his hometown. "I thought Kubo was joining us?" Cadence asked as she rode up next to him. Last she had seen the young woman, Kubo had been riding just in front of them as they left the grounds of the keep.

Rei nodded off into the distance. "She accused us of dawdling and trotted on ahead. I told her if she comes across bandits, she's on her own." The usual buoyancy in his voice was missing, taking Cadence aback.

"You're somber." Cadence guided her horse closer to his side. "I can tell the mood is more than worry. You look a bit like I do when I'm Calon bound."

"Truth? Satura is uncomfortable for me, so I don't visit it often. I haven't lived in the city's borders since I left for the Lyceum Academy before I turned 14, but it is still my sister's home, and I do miss her." His tone relayed his uneasiness. Rei turned to her and smiled. "The feeling isn't from Satura, it's the past and those that cling to it. Give it another twenty years and I'm sure it will be a welcoming place to live again."

"Arasi's lands aren't all that far from here," Cadence noted. "The Lyceum schools, they're to the east, aren't they? On the coast?"

Rei nodded. "Everything is no more than two or three days' travel from the coast to the mountains in this area."

"You don't venture out too far, huh?" Cadence aimed to distract him from whatever was bothering him.

Rei squinted in thought. "Happenstance," he stated, "these days. When I was in the Principal Regiment, we traversed the entirety of Sentan. I wasn't with them long enough to experience more, but they often train and patrol past our borders in Mora. You should be aware of that, Prime Mediator." He gave her a sidelong glance.

"Yes, well, your military background is still fresh news. You'll have to fill in some details for me," Cadence reminded him, and he shrugged in agreement.

"Did you forget that we traveled together?" Rei asked. "Was quite a far trip too."

"Of course not; it wasn't long ago. Last year? A bit north of Calon to the lovely, windy Bay of Longhowl. Mora Avi side of the water. Retrieving some special rocks for Arasi."

"Rocks?" Rei balked. "Rocks?" He shook his head. "Those were star fragments. Emanating celestial energies as much as you and I."

"I said they were special rocks, didn't I?" Cadence reiterated defensively. "They were pretty, at least."

"And powerful. And rare."

"*And* being collected by the Avi children to use in their flower gardens." She laughed.

"I would have collected them too, as a child. They glow and pulse, behave as if they are conscious. Wouldn't have realized how dangerous they were. So many stars I watched falling to earth, but they were never close enough for me to capture. Thankfully, you were able to explain their importance to the queen. Made our taking them a bit smoother." Rei's tone turned wistful as he stared up at the crisp blue sky.

Cadence clicked her tongue. "Still stealing from children, though. They didn't care about the gold we offered. Coins weren't as pretty as those special rocks." She paused. "Certainly was a good trip, though. Took, what? Almost a month there and back? I thought you'd be bored going on such an effortless mission, but you seemed to enjoy yourself."

"I did!" Rei smiled, and Cadence was relieved he finally looked at ease. "The journey was a break from Urie and running around after a new to the fold and overly enthusiastic Kubo. Sampling local dishes each night, collecting my own shiny rocks! I just wish…" His voice trailed off, and he gave a dramatic sigh.

"What?"

"Well, I just wish it hadn't been so cold once we reached Mora Avi. The way that wind came off the bay, I think my backside is still numb in spots." Cadence stared at him confused, trying to gleam what he was getting at. She could tell by his tone that he was playing at something. He waited, but she only stared back at him quizzically. "You don't remember, because you were warm." His tone was accusatory yet playful.

"You were the one next to the fire. I was behind you." She cocked her head, waiting.

"Correct. And that meant, to you, I didn't need my blanket."

"What are you going on about? I don't think I ever said that at all. I am certain I did not."

Rei let go of the reins and brought his hands to his chest, reenacting her shivers. "So cold, so cold." He mimicked her sleepy voice. "You have all the warm. *Snore*." Cadence's eyes went wide, and she shook her head. "A soft, feminine hand materialized from the air and tugged my blanket away from me. Let's switch, I offered, but no." He mimicked her sleepy voice again. "Nooo. It is too hot by the fire. *Snore*, again. I want a little warm. A little *snore* warm."

"You're exaggerating!" Cadence was mortified. "You whole-heartedly believe this fairy tale?"

His voice turned ominous as he continued. "Then, suddenly, a scooting sound against the ground, unlike any our freezing hero had ever heard. He sensed the coldness moving closer. In the dim light of the fire, he felt the icy fingers entwine the straps of his vest and their deathlike cold seep through his shirt into his skin, stealing the heat from his body. With no blanket to defend himself, there was little he could do. Alas, he gave into the cold embrace and shivered into his frigid miniature death of slumber."

Cadence could tell how proud of his storytelling skills Rei was. "Impressive how many words you came up with for being cold."

"I had a lot of time to think about it that night. Each time my eyes closed I became nervous — there was no way to tell if I was falling asleep or freezing to death."

"Remember I've said before how you can be surprisingly dreadful? Well, this is one of those times." Her face was burning from both chagrin and suppressing her laughter. "You could have woken me up and made me switch. Or taken your blanket back."

Rei bowed toward her in his saddle. "I may have been cold, but I didn't say it wasn't enjoyable." He winked. His smile widened at how fast her head turned away, and not another word was uttered. Bashfulness was not common for Cadence, and there was something satisfying witnessing that trait suddenly wash over her. Particularly when he was the cause.

*
**

Their small group reached the town of Satura limits by late afternoon. Rei pointed out a swatch of trees in the distance as they passed a crossing point on the road. "Follow that down about a mile and you will come to the center of Satura. Merchant's Row, the lodges, markets. If it were nighttime, you'd be able to observe a soft yellow glow over the trees from the lamps and square bonfire they light each night." Cadence thought his voice sounded the slightest sentimental. "Somewhere off to the side of the square is a modest shop of the finest dyes in Sentan, which was my family's. Still is, I guess." He smiled at Cadence. "Pleased? I told you something about me."

Rei's sister and her family were closer to Satura's south-western border, which meant they still had a little ways to go. The road they were on continued smooth, but since it would be more than two hours until they reached the Ona estate, they decided to stop at a tavern to rest the horses and their backsides. A meal of more than the standard dry travel food they had in their packs would also be a welcome late lunch.

The Thirsty Hoof tavern, fixed conveniently on the side of the road, seemed a suitable stop for them. The main building was much better looking than most of the taverns Cadence had patronized in her years and cleaner than most of the ones on the outskirts of Calon. The stable beside the tavern was empty, save for only two mounts, meaning they wouldn't have much of a wait if the inside was less appealing.

Before they entered, Rei pulled their small group aside. "Peaceful towns can have dodgy places too." He eyed the entrance and grimaced. "A grand establishment as this is situated far from the shops and homes for a reason: everyone needs an escape. Unfortunately, this is the only place that doesn't take us off our path. Be exceptionally soft-spoken and"—he leaned close and made direct eye contact with Kubo—"not even minor magic nor mention of. We're not wearing our caster robes for a reason."

Settling in at a table near the front door in the sparsely populated room, it didn't take long for Cadence to understand why Rei had given them their lecture; obvious glares thrown their direction and the hostility was tangible. "Is it because they recognize casters? Or that we're Calon guards?" she asked Kubo as Rei gathered the food from the tavern keeper. Most of the continent spoke a common language, with only slight variations, but the patrons at the tavern were older and speaking exclusively Sentan. This wasn't uncommon, and Cadence had a basic grasp of the language, but she couldn't keep up with the pace and accent of the dialect in Satura, though.

"Um, no." Kubo shook her head. The caster sat in quiet concentration for a moment, her expression pained. She didn't travel the area much and wasn't familiar with the townspeople, but the sentiment in the room was obvious. "It's not us at all. Comments about dark magic of some sort, I don't understand, but the hostility is all directed at Rei?" Fluent in both languages as all Sentan were, the apprentice was still as lost as Cadence. "They're being, I'm not sure how to explain it. Antagonistic? They aren't speaking to him but to each other *about* him." Her face turned sad. "They are loud because they want him to hear but too afraid to say it to his face." The young woman shook her head. "Something is off."

Cadence studied the room once more. The tavern didn't give off an air of hostility as others in less respectable communities did, but she was travel wise enough to know that wasn't always an accurate indicator. "Satura is his hometown. People here would be aware that he was a caster, so it isn't something Rei can disguise. I thought druids and their adjuncts were more respected than this."

"They are," Kubo told her quietly. "At least, overall. Some people believe certain casters use their skills for self-gain and malevolent antics. They aren't wrong, that does happen, but not nearly as much as people like to pretend, and never with a druid connected to the royal family. Usually, they only harbor those thoughts after they've witnessed such trickery. That's why their energy is directed at Rei and not us."

Cadence grimaced. "Seems grossly misplaced."

"We're of the same mind, then. I don't like these people." Kubo's voice turned uncharacteristically cold. "I'd like to turn them tongue-tied for a few days."

"Can you do that?" Cadence whispered. Kubo's silver eyes gleamed as she gave an almost imperceptible nod, and Cadence thought for a moment how delightful that would be.

Rei came back to the table with a tray of bread, cheese, and a lone tomato sliced into the thinnest of slivers, as well as a pitcher of water. "They are conveniently out of meats or wine or fruit," he told them, doubt filling his voice. "Everything they did provide looks decent enough. Mika will make sure we have a fulfilling dinner tonight, so this should be a fine placeholder."

"Why are they so rude to you here?" Kubo piped up before Rei was in his seat. She couldn't fathom her teacher making enemies with anyone, and the hostility inside the tavern burned her heart.

Rei shrugged, unfazed, and shoved a chunk of cheese into his mouth. "The quakes have every person in Sentan anxious, and they likely think the druids aren't doing enough to help." He kept his voice soft and low, but his eyes stayed alert, constantly scanning the room. "Anyone who remembers me is aware I serve Arasi, so…" He let that statement hang. "I said we aren't to discuss these things. Let's eat and carry on out of here."

Kubo glanced around nervously. "They're still talking about you, though. I know you hear them."

"Get used to it, apprentice," Rei ordered. "Learn to eat fast and not make eye contact. We don't cause problems, we fix them, no matter what they want to believe." Kubo went to say more, but Rei held up his hand. "Eat."

Their group had only been sitting a few minutes and were finishing their skimpy meal when Cadence felt Rei tap her arm and lean toward her. "Cadence, dismiss your guards to the stable and have them ready their horses." His voice was barely audible, and for a moment she wondered if he had spoken out loud or into her head. No sooner had she followed Rei's directions and her guards left the table when a graying, middle-aged man, with what once may have been a charming smile, approached them.

Eyeing each of them and nodding respectfully to Cadence, the man placed his hands on the table, directly across from Rei. "You're strangers here, aren't you? Welcome to Satura." His voice was friendlier than his eyes let on. His gaze landed on Rei, and they stared at one another expressionless for a long moment. "Though some are not as welcome as others." The man moved forward and knocked one of the mugs of water onto Rei. Cadence went to stand, but Rei shot a hand behind her, pulling Cadence back into the seat by her jacket and continued to hold her in place. He shot her a quick look that silenced any question she had. The man sneered, proud of what he had done. "Do they know what your magic is used for?"

Rei pursed his lips. "Magic could be used to contain that vile mouth of yours. Rid the tavern of whatever stench I've been smelling. Seems that's probably you." Rei looked the man up and down and shook his head. "You've really let yourself go, old man." The man lit into Rei with a series of obviously angry Sentan words, which made Kubo flinch, but his stance made it obvious that he was hesitant to get into a physical row with the caster. Rei's hand was still on Cadence's back, and though his face relayed only calm, his muscles were rigid and prepared to fight. She didn't know at that point if he were holding her or himself back. With the man still snarling insults, she felt Rei drop his hand and pat her back.

"Kubo, gather the food. We're leaving." Rei stood and held up his hands to the man, who abruptly yelled and backed away, enraged that Rei might get too close. "Well, this was a pleasurable Satura welcome. I see not much has changed. We'll be going." Rei turned and said something to the man in Sentan that Cadence couldn't understand, but the shocked look on Kubo's face told her it must have been an appropriate response to their exchange.

Rei herded them out of the door as the man continued his rant. Empowered by what was unfolding, others from the tavern joined in the taunting. They had made it to the other side of the door of the tavern without further incident when the man yelled louder than before, and Cadence distinctly heard Rei's name along with the Sentan word for 'father.' She stopped cold and turned, just as the man attempted to spit on Rei, and without thinking, drew her arm back to strike. Cadence never got the chance; her fist connected with air as she watched her target moving away from her, or her moving away from her target. Rei had sensed her turn and, swifter than she thought humanly possible, had snatched her up and thrown her over his shoulder before she started a brawl and carried her calmly down the porch steps. Behind them, the patrons cackled as they shuffled back to their drinks.

"What are you doing?" Cadence demanded. "Put me down! You can't let that stand! I'll deal with them if you won't!"

"Nope. You most certainly will not. It's all fine. Some of the townsfolk are a little off. A common tragedy. That charming fellow is Hanto. I've been dealing with him since I was a kid. Doesn't often come this far out of the town square, so he was probably on a drinking binge. Certainly reeked of something. He's nothing to start a fight over. Leftover strife from my youth, but it's nothing to worry about."

Once they reached the stable, Rei dropped her and smiled, but Cadence recognized he was unsettled.

"If I am not worried about it, you are not to worry about it. Understood?" Rei patted her head as though she were a child, and Cadence swatted his hand away.

"I understand that you would not want myself or another Calon to intervene—it is not our business. Still, you or Kubo should have at least put him in his place. I'm not saying with magic or much violence." Cadence tried to say it as calmly as possible, but the entire exchange had her heated.

Rei fidgeted with the reins of his horse. "And what would you have had us do? Cause an incident to encourage more of those types of exchanges?" His tone was icy. "I have done enough fighting here and put more than enough people in their place when I was in Principal. Whether it's with a blade or a spell, I'm not taking that path again. The people have trust issues they need to sort out. I learned a long time ago that it is on them, not me, not us." Rei gave Cadence a stern look, and the displeasure in his eyes caught her off guard. "And you know better, Prime Mediator, than to become involved or give in to such behavior. We've both been trained in such matters. Where are your Calon diffusion techniques?" Noticing the repentant look on her face, Rei's expression softened. "It's behind us. So we carry on, lest we get held back. Right?" He scratched his head and smirked. "And Kubo? You think Kubo could have done something? Kubo would have let her enthusiasm get the best of her and collapsed the tavern. Then the stable. Possibly the entire countryside."

The flush in Cadence's face refused to dissipate as she took Rei's words in. He was unequivocally correct; she'd let her emotions get the best of her.

Still, she wasn't regretful. "I didn't like the way he was treating you."

"Which is why I don't live here anymore in the first place. Uncomfortable, remember?" Rei forced a tight-lipped smile as he handed her one of the sacks Kubo had hurriedly thrust their food into. "Divide these up as you see fit. When we reach the Ona estates, the spread there will more than make up for the missed meal here." Despite the questions burning her tongue, Cadence acquiesced.

Mika, Rei's younger sister, was jubilant when they arrived at her home and embraced each of them, even the guards. Cadence had expected that she would follow Rei's attribute of purple hair, but her golden curls showed it was not a common familial trait. Mika did, however, match her brother's kind and jovial attitude. Her husband, Regi, would be back the day after next and would be honored to help them with Arasi's questions, she assured them. The quakes and disruption of the trade routes had the citizens concerned, and any investigation was welcome. Until then, the estate was theirs to wander and relax.

As they settled in for dinner, Mika's promise to tour the vineyard grounds the next morning spurred Cadence's curiosity. Strictly in the spirit of gathering intelligence, she hoped she could persuade Mika to share more details on Rei than he ever did himself. Or, at least shed some light on what had transpired at the inn.

Chapter Eight

Breakfast in Satura was traditionally served before the sun was fully risen, but Mika didn't mind letting her guests sleep in. Rei, however, was not a guest. She prodded her brother awake early to help. As children, she had been the one Rei jostled awake to aid in preparing breakfast, so she enjoyed watching him struggle to wipe the sand from his eyes now. He'd gotten too used to his spoiled life with Binder Arasi. Rei didn't mind as much as he feigned, and together they created a buffet of classic Sentan options.

After everyone had eaten and the food settled a bit, Mika made good on her promise to show the group around. The tour of the Ona family estate and vineyard was lengthy, and Rei joined them for a part of it before excusing himself discretely before lunch. He had been to the estate many times and instead opted to set up the maps in the study for later.

Cadence was certain there was more to it, he'd been quieter than usual, but didn't press him, considering what had happened earlier. Instead, she took the opportunity to casually question Mika about Rei when Kubo and her guards were out of earshot. His sister relished the chance to share some of Rei's life with Cadence.

"Your brother is remarkably calm and kind. It's hard to imagine him being in the Sentan Principal Regiment. That doesn't seem like a good fit for him," Cadence told Mika as they walked through the vineyard. The tepid climate of Sentan had given them a sunny but cool day, and the workers were happily chatting as they picked at the grapes that were added to the plum juice. "In Calon, the members of the disciplined ranks are usually born from hatred or discontent."

"Rei's not unfamiliar with such emotions. Though, the only person Rei has ever hated, that I am aware of at least, has been himself."

Cadence frowned. "That conflicts so much with the Rei I've spent time with."

Mika nodded. "If you aren't seeing that, then that is a positive thing. That means he's come a long way." They walked on farther and came to a shaded area with tables and chairs. "This is a good spot for lunch," the younger woman announced. Mika instructed the workers to bring samples out for their guests and asked everyone to make themselves comfortable. She waved Cadence to a table a bit away from the others and continued telling her about their childhood.

"I'm not saying Rei wasn't happy. His mood ebbed and flowed, but I've since learned that's how it is with most young people, now that I have gone through the stages with my own children." Mika smiled. "Growing up, Rei was happiest at night, though. He was always outside chasing firebugs and the dartbirds that would come out after dusk. Sometimes they would chase him back or sit on the ledges waiting for him to come play. He would smuggle some of father's parchments and ink out with him and draw the sky. He even gave each star a name and pointed out where each was every night, though he denies that now."

Mika's voice softened and sounded almost sad. "Mother once said Rei was 'bound to the stars more than our family.' I remember more than a few mornings when she or father would find him burrowed in blankets on the grass next to our home and carry him back to his bed. For a while, mother used to pin his pictures to the ceiling above our beds, so Rei could sleep under his sky even on rainy nights. I think at night, Rei had no one to bother him, and he could let his thoughts be unrestrained. Practice his tricks without an audience. He had magic talents from a young age and that made him a target for the adults to try and force their will."

"Bonding with the stars. He was trending druidic, not caster. Do you think that's why Rei started hiding his abilities?" Cadence asked.

"Partly. Druidic power comes with a great deal of expectation in Sentan, as I'm sure you're aware of. No doubt that gave him an air of melancholy. Rei liked the attention, wanted to share his abilities, but my brother was trying to find his way without being molded by others. No one wants to let a child think for themselves. I've been guilty of that with my own children." She smiled wistfully. "I think a turning point was when Rei got into a fight with an older child who had been breaking my toys. That was the first time he had gotten into a physical scrap, and Rei flattened him." Mika's eyes lit up at the memory. "After that, Rei fell into the protector role; not just for me but for a few of the other children. It made him happier, and that became his calling. He believed Regiment training would give him the ability to help more people, protect others. Protect himself more, yet."

"He might have done that as a caster as well." Cadence paused as the wine was served and thanked her hostess. "Perhaps even as a druid. Arasi believes that Rei can still do that. In his place," she continued.

"I am certain of it," Mika agreed. "If he felt being a druid suited him, he would do amazing things with it." She excused herself to make sure that the others were taken care of, then returned, pulling her chair closer to Cadence. "What about you, Prime Mediator?"

Cadence wasn't certain how to respond. "I haven't much to talk about."

"That's not true. Rei's mentioned you several times over the years, so there must be something. Let's see… aside from the whole Calon representative position, he's mentioned you're weak at pachi but are a skilled artist and is impressed with your fighting abilities. That last one impresses him, but as with Rei, I can't imagine what would draw you to that."

"My choice was more of a defensive move," Cadence explained. "And later, my escape from my version of being molded. My family changed their expectations for me after I'd already started my path. This was the direction that let me retain who I was." She felt the sympathy in Mika's stare and shook her head. "It wasn't my initial goal, but it has led me on some great adventures over the years. Not my first choice, but I cannot deny it was by far the best choice."

"I understand that quite well," Mika sympathized. "Seeing Rei accepted to the Lyceum Paths made me think about what I wanted, even if our parents didn't approve. They had wanted someone to pass their shop on to, and it wouldn't be to the one off fighting across the continent. I didn't like the idea of being fixed indoors." She smiled. "Rei had his stars, and I had my dirt. So I played with plants, met a boy who played with plants, and left to play in the best, richest dirt in Sentan. Our cousins inherited our family shop when our parents passed away a few years ago. They preferred coins to stars and dirt, so it was a better fit." She laughed.

Cadence laughed with her. "It's nice to discover these things, to learn about your family. Getting any information out of Rei is challenging, to say the least. I only found out about you a few days before we left to come here. And I only found out he was in the Principal Regiment because I saw his markings the other night."

"Oh?" Mika raised her eyebrows and grinned.

"Oh! Not anything inappropriate," Cadence blurted, realizing how her comment sounded. She felt her cheeks turning red. "We were in the springs and—well, never mind. It won't sound good no matter how I explain it." They both laughed, and her embarrassment turned to amusement.

"So what about your family? Parents? Siblings? Pets?"

Cadence shrugged. "My parents are a lost cause, but I was never close to them, just grandparents. They have been gone for a long time now, though. I have a cousin and his children, another cousin somewhere. Otherwise, friends, the guards in my company. Arasi makes an amusing pet."

"Sounds like Rei isn't the only one who doesn't like to share details about themselves." Mika raised an eyebrow.

"I'm sorry. You've been so gracious and allowed me to learn much about your family. I'm not trying to be rude. You become comfortable living behind doors. Sometimes you don't know how to open them even though they aren't locked."

Mika moved closer and took Cadence's hands in hers, appearing to be the older one of the two in her demeanor. Her smile was bright and welcoming, and Cadence relaxed. "You sound like someone else in my life." She leaned back and poured the last of the wine into their small glasses. "Not many from Calon come here"—she kindly changed the subject—"you must like Sentan."

"Greatly," Cadence admitted. "Amazing to me how much more comfortable I am here than at home. The land has a warmth that has nothing to do with the weather."

"Our people."

"I'm certain." She smiled. "The way it is here is more reminiscent of where I grew up, my childhood home. It was outside the main cities, away from the hustle and bustle. The people here are warmer, friendlier. They appreciate different things, embrace new ideas. Except some…" Cadence hesitated, uncertain if Mika was aware of the incident at the tavern.

"Except some people," she finished for her, and Cadence nodded. "No place is perfect. You've traveled enough to have encountered what I'm speaking of. Not every person is gifted with empathy or understanding, even if they have what passes for intelligence. There will always be those who make a conscious effort to not understand." Mika gathered the glasses and plates from their table into a neat pile. "I see no reason this can't be your home too."

Cadence took her words to heart. "You're kind. I do find it lovely here, and I wouldn't rule it out one day, when things are calm."

"I've been to Calon on a few trips and have no complaints," Mika told her, though her voice sounded unconvincing. "Took the route along the Poltan coast, and it was an amazing journey. In all honesty, returning to Sentan was the best part of the trip."

Mika began to lead them back to the house. "Why are you so curious about my brother?" she suddenly asked, catching an unsuspecting Cadence off guard. Her smile was warm though, and Cadence shook off her embarrassment.

She thought of a hundred responses that would conceal the truth but settled for honesty. "Rei makes me happy when so few others do. As such, I want to learn more about him."

Mika nodded. "That's always come easy for him, making others happy. The hard part is making Rei happy."

"Despite the current situation, he acts as though he is."

"I'm sure he is, when *you* see him." Mika's amusement was obvious, and a slow realization came over Cadence that the younger woman was not teasing her so much as subtly playing matchmaker. It made her wonder just how much Rei had shared with her, or if Arasi had planned this in advance.

*
**

The group reconvened for dinner as twilight darkened the sky. The mood around the table was jovial, and Kubo delighted in showing Mika some simple tricks Rei had taught her.

Afterwards, Cadence and the guards retired to the common parlor while the brother and sister helped the servants clean up.

Mika was making the chore list for the day servants when Rei came into the pantry and began poking around shelves.

"Take some plum wine and sweet biscuits to your companions. They might make for a nice light treat before sleep." She smiled and touched Rei's shoulder as he brushed past. "It's cute."

"What is?" Rei asked as he scooped some mugs into a basket, along with the biscuits.

"The way that you and she steal glimpses at one another. You do realize there are other people in the room when you do that, yes?" Rei didn't respond. "Or where your eyes go when she—"

"Mika!"

"Don't be embarrassed. You're both adults, and she does it too." She ignored the pout her brother was giving her and continued. "You like her. Me too. I approve."

He shrugged and added a bottle of wine to the basket. "I've known her for a few years now, so of course we're fond," Rei explained, remembering what Urie had said. "Nothing more. Currently."

"Fond," his sister repeated. "What an odd word to use." She smiled at Rei as she added some additional biscuits to the bunch and eyed the basket. "Interesting you're taking only two mugs when I counted eight members in your party."

Rei casually put the basket down onto the counter and sighed, having been caught before he realized it himself. "The Calon guards don't drink wine, and Kubo has been asleep for an hour already."

Mika shook her head and smiled. "Cadence was asking a lot of questions about you earlier. About your life here." She paused as Rei visibly tensed up. "If you hope for it to be more than fondness, then you need to be open with her. Cadence told me how trying it is to get anything out of you. That's what you always do. So change that. Maybe even tonight." Mika brushed the misbehaving strands of purple out of her brother's eyes. "If you are going to bury the past, you have to stop visiting the grave. Instead, you let it hold you prisoner, chained inside a cell because of what might happen."

"Because of what did happen," Rei corrected her. "What continues to happen."

Mika lovingly stared up into her brother's eyes and recognized the fear hidden behind them. "I only want you out of that prison once and for all. You now seem to have found someone with a key. Tell them how to open it."

Rei was stoic and uncharacteristically solemn. "And if I do tell her and she no longer looks at me the same?"

Mika hugged him with all the strength she could muster in hopes of squashing his doubts. "You don't have to say anything you don't want to, you only have to say what you need to. If that is enough to push her away, then, she doesn't deserve your love." She said, annunciating her last word. "Now go. I saw the rest of the guards retire to their room earlier, so I knew what you were up to." Her brother glared at her as he backed out of the pantry, but a slight smile showed on his lips. Mika hummed to herself as she cleaned the countertops and headed to her chambers.

Rei carried the basket into the vestibule where the main fireplace was. Only Cadence was in the room now, reviewing her notes on the floor by the firelight.

"Everyone's gone to sleep." She looked up at Rei. "Poor, weary soldiers, exhausted from a day spent touring a vineyard and eating sweets. Speaking of, did you bring treats?" She smiled hopefully at the basket.

Her smile was luminous, and Rei's heart sank to think that his words might take that sight from him forever. He plopped down on a cushion across from her and set the basket between them.

"It just so happens that I did. Mika's biscuits complement the wine superbly. They're also tasty on their own. She used to make a huge batch of them for me to take to school each season, and they never made it a week." Rei made himself as comfortable as possible and sighed. "I heard Mika was boring you with stories about our childhood."

"At least one of you is forthcoming." Cadence grinned and closed her journal. "It was great to finally get a little piece of your history."

"You should probably hear my side too. Seems only fair."

Cadence recognized the melancholy on Rei's face. She bent forward and placed her hand on his. "You don't have to say anything. Listening to Mika's stories was captivating. It was refreshing to learn that you are more than some caster with secret military training." She took a sip of the wine. "Much better than that swill Arasi drinks!"

"Eh, he only drinks that swill because Ki-tae loves it." Surprising himself, Rei boldly took her hand fully in his. "Growing up here was fine, it's that even under the best circumstances you don't always fit in, and that becomes an inconvenience to people. Some didn't like me for that very reason—and apparently still don't—such as Hanto, the fun gentleman from the tavern. Because they remember the old me, the me I was born as, the me they knew as a child. Not the me that I became." He paused then and smiled warmly. "For the record, I was pretty amazing, from childhood up to now. You can absolutely put that in your notes." Cadence nodded in agreement, staring up at him intently with her dark-green eyes. For a moment, Rei became lost in them; he'd never seen a shade as hers, like juniper, and regret began to creep icily up his spine. He blinked and continued in spite of it.

Rei released her hand and settled against the wall behind him. "When I lived here with Mika, I was…" He searched for the words in the common language they all shared, which made it difficult; it was a more straightforward language than Sentan, and the descriptions he knew didn't always make sense to interpret. "Mika didn't always have…" He hesitated and stared upward, searching for the words as though they could be found written on the ceiling. Rei remembered what Cadence had told him about deflecting conversations away from himself and realized he was doing that even now. "A brother."

Rei let out a heavy breath. "I was born different than I appear now. Well, not really. There was a bit of a disconnect, to make use of a word Arasi had once given me for it." He stopped, his mouth dry, waiting for the look of bewilderment to cloud Cadence's face. Her expression didn't change though, and she cocked her head, waiting for him to continue. "Some people remember that version, cling to it. They are under the impression that this version of me is all a lie, a caster illusion. Or, as my mother had once claimed, caused by cracking my skull too many times during Regiment training." Rei shook his head. "Which was ludicrous considering my agility." He tried to find humor, but it didn't materialize. "I'm not explaining well."

"You are," Cadence assured him.

"I'm not," Rei disagreed, and his uneasiness tore at her heart. "The words I need are not forthcoming."

"If the words escape you, then, let them. That means they aren't the right ones anyway. You don't have to—"

"But I do," he interrupted, "because…" If he were already uncomfortable, he might as well go all the way to the edge. "I value your belief and trust in me. If you learn things from others that place doubt in—"

"Rei, I don't think it's possible to have doubts about you." Cadence reached over and took the biscuit out of Rei's hand for herself, hoping to distract him. He flashed her an expression of mock offense, and his heavy mood broke for a moment. "If there is more you want to explain, I will gladly listen. If the words hurt, then I'd rather sit here in silence with you."

Beholden to her kindness, Rei stared down at the oak floorboards and then reached for his mug, knowing the wine wouldn't quench the dryness in his mouth. "I appreciate that. Anything you want to ask?" Rei had answered so many questions about his past in his life and didn't like the idea of them coming from the woman he was not so secretly in love with.

Cadence shook her head. "I only want to listen to whatever you want to tell me." Her eyes were genuine, and the warmth of comfort came back to Rei. Her trust in him was tangible.

"When I was admitted to the Lyceum Academy for Regiment, I had more freedom to be who I wanted. I was able to grow into myself without the expectations of others. At the academies, no one cared, so long as you followed code and excelled at your path. Which I did." Rei poured more wine into his mug, though it wasn't empty—not from thirst but rather nerves. "Coming home between seasons, that was, uh, definitely an undertaking, to put it mildly. Only Mika was indifferent. When she was older, we talked about those times. She said that she didn't notice because that was how she always saw me. There was no dissimilarity to her." Rei smiled, and Cadence could see the love and gratitude reflected in his face. "After a while, it wasn't comfortable coming home. The more I changed, or rather refused to change, the more the stares turned to name calling and occasionally worse. For the good things here, and I promise there are, it wasn't worth it. Not for me. Not at that time in my life.

"After I completed studies, I ascended to a sanctioned Regiment. Less years than it had taken others, and I promise you, not one touch of magic assisted me." He smiled proudly. "I kept that a secret as well— my other concern. Promotion to Principal Regiment wasn't all that long after." He pointed to his arm where the markings were under his shirt. "No one knew me as anyone other than Rei. That was relieving, but not being fully who I was, keeping part of me secret, wore at my heart. I still can't uncover the right words for how I was feeling then. Angry? Frustrated? Eager? Exhausted? After so many years of hiding myself, I knew that I was done questioning. So I took up the challenge to make things more permanent, so to speak."

"You sought out the druids then?" Cadence asked. Druidic magic was born of the elements; transition was part of their abilities on a vast number of levels.

Rei shook his head. "Where I was assigned, it was remote. Aside from a small unit of casters, magic users of any sort were not present. Without question, no druids. Or so I thought." He grimaced. "One night, I sat out and thought among the stars as I often did and decided it was a task I should put on myself."

"Alone?" Now Cadence's expression did change, to one of concern.

Rei nodded. "Normally it would require higher experience, but all I had was myself and the stars. My trust in the stars had never failed me before."

"That's why the druids took an interest," Cadence remarked. "Focusing that amount of magic into itself, the energy would have been sensed for miles. Even casters would have felt it. You shouldn't have been strong enough to do that alone—almost no one is, not even Arasi. Such an incantation is complicated at best and at worst…" She stared into the fire. "You may have died."

"Oh, quite messily. To be honest, at that time in my life, that was a viable option for me. I had nothing else." His voice was very matter of fact. Cadence frowned at his words, but it was an important truth. A long moment of silence clung to them, broken only by the crackling fire. "Though, it's been quite a long time now, and everything appears to have been successful!" Rei's usual demeanor returned.

Cadence smiled. "You seem happy."

"I am." He sincerely was, especially at that moment, sitting across from her.

"I still don't understand why you tried to forsake your magic abilities, even after that. It was proof of your skills, and we both know that's above caster level. You said you liked the challenge better, but you could easily become a druid. Harnessing such skills, you would surpass Arasi instead of only assisting him." Cadence thought back to the night the druid had called Rei his proxy, and it made sense now. "It's glaringly obvious you have the ability, and Arasi won't be around forever. I'm sure that—"

Rei put up his hands. "No chance." He gave a tight-lipped grin. "I want nothing more than this." He took a drink. "Less responsibility, more quiet fireside drinks. Biscuits." He paused. "If I change my mind in the future, you will be among the first to hear about it."

"I understand. No one wants to be forced into something they don't want, though it may be the right fit. Well, what others think is the right fit. Does seem a waste of talent though, if you ask me." Cadence paused for a moment, then frowned. "I'm sorry if you felt you had to share. I wasn't trying to pry. You didn't have to."

"I'm aware." Rei smiled. "I chose to. Uncomfortable as it is at the start, I find that having this conversation is easier when done by choice and not by necessity, so to speak. My past has caused some discord with those I felt strongly about, and I'd like to not experience that again." Cadence caught his choice of words and smiled.

"Besides, you saw firsthand today that occasionally it still ruffles people, and if you are going to be around me, then it makes sense that you know." Rei sighed. "Arasi thinks I let it hold me back, but he doesn't understand the reasons as intimately as I do. Means well, though."

"He does," she agreed, "but he lives in his own world. Actually, I do have a question."

"Ask away."

She eyed the top of his head. "Your hair…"

"Hey! I love this hair!" He protectively put his hands on his head before she finished her question. "I wouldn't change that for the world! I think this purple is my favorite feature. Though, it does need some cutting, but we've been a bit busy."

"Well, no doubt you are easy to find in a crowd." Cadence laughed. "I am only teasing. It's one of my favorite features of yours too."

For a few moments, they were quiet and comfortable. They munched on biscuits and stared into the fire.

"Our friend back at the tavern, Hanto, we grew up together. Hatred and drinking have aged him beyond his years, but he was the shining star of his family house—celebrated for following each order. I wanted that as well, and for a short moment, I did bend to those expectations, pushing what I wanted aside. When you're young and don't know any better, you crave to please the people you love before yourself. It wasn't until later that I saw what those expectations did to him. It helped me to not regret my choices." Rei sat back with a sad smile. He wasn't pleased to see where Hanto's life had taken him.

"Regretting the past sets up the future for disappointment. It's not a healthy place to live."

Cadence slid over beside him and offered a biscuit. She took his arm and put her head on his shoulder, and Rei inclined his head down to rest on hers. They sat in silence for a while, the snapping of the fire and crunching of the biscuits the only sounds. The wine, coupled with the warmth of the room and comfort of being next to Rei, began to make her sleepy.

"Thank you"—Cadence looked up at Rei—"for letting me learn about you."

"Thank you for wanting to, and for understanding. I hope you took plenty of notes," he teased. "I'm sorry it took so long to share. Trust is still something I struggle with." She was strikingly beautiful in the firelight, and the warmth of her softness against him calmed him. He ached to kiss her then but banished the thought, the slightest sting of past pain still pulling him back. "So, when do I get to be captivated with stories of your life?"

"I suppose that's fair, isn't it?" Cadence stood and yawned. "I will warn you now, the wine won't be as tasty in Calon." She reached down and tousled his hair. "Good night, Rei."

Chapter Nine

The following morning, the company reconvened for breakfast, and the mood was light. Mika had dismissed the servants for the day so that she could indulge her guests herself, with Rei's assistance. "Your talk must have gone well," Mika remarked quietly as they cleared the table after. "She's still looking at you the same way."

"Our talk was fine." Rei smiled without adding another word. He didn't need to; his relaxed tone spoke volumes.

Regi Ona arrived later that morning. A brawny man a few years younger than Mika, he mirrored her kind and pleasant character. Though their unannounced visit concerned him, Regi was far from anxious about the circumstances. Citizens from the area, predominately those who worked the vineyards, knew the instability had been growing, but they hadn't been aware of how far reaching the chaos was. The vintner took lunch alone with Mika to gather his thoughts before asking Cadence and her group into the study. Grove Mistress Shon joined them.

The soil used for the family's vineyard came from the base of the mountain chain along Sentan's southern border. Regi explained that mining in the area had uncovered a series of ancient lava conduits, which ran beneath their orchards and vineyards. He indicated several points on the map. "These three gold markings are active, but the ones in red have become too unstable to risk going down into." Regi asked Shon to explain their process and stepped aside.

"Our excavators go into the mines to retrieve the soil several times a month. Quakes in the area have increased in length and intensity, making it an almost impossible task now. The support walls of the mines are growing increasingly unstable, and we don't want to put anyone at risk, so excavation work has ceased." She pointed to a black spot along the mountains in the north of Sentan. "A few months ago, officers from the mining league alerted us this former mine had collapsed. We thought it was odd it would fall before the ones here." Shon trailed her fingers down the map.

"Why so?" Cadence asked.

"That mine was modern, only active in recent years and not as far dug down as the ones here. The southern mountains are volcanic in birth, and rumblings are part of their character." She shrugged. "But to the north, those mountains are static, and instability is historically rare for them. When we added it to our map for reference, it became obvious that the mines to the north and west were collapsing, almost in succession."

Regi tapped the map. "Starting on the northern coast and going southwest. None of ours have collapsed, but the mines we are cautious about are the ones that would have been along that path."

"We have no additional collapsed mines," Shon continued, "but if you continue the path westward, that's where the landslides and sinkholes are being reported."

Cadence nodded. "Along the trade routes."

"The vegetation along the routes is withering away despite plentiful water. Plant life doesn't want to grow." Regi's voice was grim. "I asked the emperor to send a survey team into our mines last year, when the quakes started occurring with greater frequency. He sent a contingent along with Binder Ki-Maris into the conduits." Binder Ki-Maris was an earth druid, which explained Arasi sending them, Cadence thought to herself and glanced at Rei.

"They revealed," Shon told them, "that the northern sections of the conduits, as far as they could safely go, were not as dense as before. I was confused as well—mining isn't my area of expertise. According to Binder Ki-Maris, walls of dirt that were once two miles thick were now one mile. In areas not common to land shifts."

Regi shook his head. "The discovery was distressing and left us confused. We realized it was only the beginning of what else was to come, so we stayed patient."

"If the emperor knows this already, why are we here getting the same information" Cadence asked.

"The maps have only been recently updated," Regi offered. "We didn't have this exact information when Binder Ki-Maris was here."

"Interesting he didn't send him back then." She shrugged.

Rei spoke up. "Binder Ki-Maris hasn't been seen in months. He was surveying the sinkhole that damaged part of Mora Tanis. He and his senior-adjunct, Kurus, were assumed lost. I don't believe anything malicious was the cause—it's well known the risks faced putting ourselves in those areas. But at the same time, something doesn't seem right with this. I walked the grounds when we first arrived, while Mika had you distracted. The pulling is consistent around Sentan but stronger here and flowing instead of pulsing. In some places, it felt as though I was on the ocean instead of the land." Rei shook his head. "My guess is that I'd perceive it profusely worse closer to Mora Tanis."

An independent trade city at the center of the continent, Mora Tanis was governed by both the countries of Firtan to the north and Poltan to the south. Between the ease of access, rich landscape, and vast gathering of merchants, it was a traveler's paradise. The surrounding perimeter and the nearby riverbank were densely populated, making any land shifts deadly to entire communities. Emperor Ki-tae had sent Binder Ki-Maris to explore a way to stop what was happening and prevent any loss of life.

Cadence examined the notes she had taken and studied the map. "We have two situations here, then. The first being: what is causing this? I think that's what Emperor Ki-tae was attempting to find out. Binder Arasi has been studying this as well for some time. But that is an afterthought for now. What's more important, which the emperor was also aware of, is the impact this can cause to Mora's inhabitants along this route. Aside from creating a valley of sorts, what other damage might we anticipate?"

Rei stretched out his arms to either end of the map. "Appears the origin is along the northeastern coast. Depending how fast and deep the split happens, we aren't looking at a valley. We'd be looking at a river. One that will come rushing up like a tidal wave and flood the surrounding lands."

"Lovely," Cadence sighed. "I don't think any of us realized the direness of the situation. A change of this scope hasn't happened in centuries." She stared at the map, but nothing more came to mind. "We think that's a strong possibility, then? The continent cracks with a sundering of wet fury?"

"In all likelihood, yes," Regi answered. "It can't be stopped if that's what is happening. Not at this point. Not with all of the druid magic in Sentan."

"Then, we can take measures to lessen the damage—that may be the best we can hope for," Cadence said. Where would the people go, and if they would heed any warning, was a question she couldn't comment on at that moment. It might mean casualties if the divide happened faster than they anticipated, or it might mean hundreds of lives lost and families separated. A summit of all leaders needed to be arranged, but contacting each one would take time they weren't certain they had; they would need to move.

The news was urgent, and Cadence didn't want to waste time by waiting for morning. "The emperor and Binder Arasi need this information without delay."

Voicing his agreement, Regi urged her to take the maps as well and asked his servants to arrange her departure.

Rei insisted on accompanying her on an immediate return to Arasi's keep. Kubo and the rest of the Calon guards would leave at first light with the additional maps and notes Regi had supplied.

*
**

Rei and Cadence rode through most of the night, with a quick midnight stop to rest their horses and eat what Mika had packed them. What Rei had shared about the effect of the land and how he believed the entirety of Mora would be even more impacted hit her in the gut. Cadence knew Rei actively hid his intuitiveness; for him to share what he sensed meant something substantial was brewing.

"What you felt about the land, the pulling you mentioned, it's more critical than you let on, isn't it?" she asked as they sat shoulder to shoulder with only half a moon to break the darkness. It was after midnight, and the land was quiet except for the heavy breathing of their exhausted horses.

"It isn't any more critical now than before," Rei responded. "But now that we have a greater understanding of what's happening, we can act on it."

"I understand that, but what you said, how you said it. You don't often sound worried."

"My worries are targeted," he replied, and Cadence made out the littlest hint of a smile in the dark, and it comforted her. "I don't distribute them rashly. But yes, in this case, there is worry, and I cannot tell you or anyone otherwise. It isn't even worrying about what is happening, so much as it is worrying about the actions—no." Rei paused and corrected himself. "Worry on the reactions. People generally aren't notorious for doing well with change, and how we act and how they react doesn't sit well in my gut."

"A well-placed worry," Cadence agreed. "Mora is the only home we have right now. We wouldn't have anywhere else to go."

"Our distant neighbors haven't proved welcoming, have they?" Rei chuckled. "I mean, aside from those of us from Sentan, when Sentasiev still existed."

Cadence stared into the dying fire. "What if that is the fate of this land as well?" She turned her head to Rei, waiting for his response. "Are we next for that destruction, but with nowhere to go? Do we need a fleet of ships to create floating cities like we've read in childhood fables?"

Rei shook his head. "No. That's not what I feel, not what Arasi feels."

"Would you tell me otherwise?" Cadence held her hands out to the darkness. "It's just us, the horses, and the flora. You know me better than to distrust me with the truth."

"It isn't a matter of trust; I wouldn't belittle you with lies, even well-meaning ones. What is happening here compared to what did happen to Sentasiev isn't of the same magnitude." The destruction of the original homeland of the Sentans, before Mora became their refuge, loomed large in everyone's thoughts on what was happening now.

"You weren't there then, nor was Arasi. How would you recognize what that feeling even is?"

"A challenge, isn't it?"

"What is?"

"Not believing that things will always turn out for the worse." He smiled at her. "Besides, if our only witnesses tonight are the horses and the flora, I'd rather waste my time doing other things than talking about the end of the world."

"Oh?" Cadence tilted her head. "*Waste* your time?"

Rei blinked, caught off guard in mid, horribly timed, flirtation. "Uh… no."

"Being with me is only one of a variety of ways you can waste your time. I see how it is." Cadence stood and stretched, staring down at him.

"I have no defense for this." Rei conceded to her teasing.

"Besides"—Cadence bent down and brushed the hair from his face—"we're both too tired to be any good at wasting time right now." She grinned and stood back up. "We need to be on our way. Why don't you extinguish what's left of the fire while I pay a quick visit to a bush?"

They remounted and broke into a brisk pace. The ride from that point would be on even ground until they reached the woods surrounding Arasi's keep, and they would make good time if they kept a steady pace.

Cadence and Rei arrived on the druid's grounds as the dawn lightened the sky. Arasi and the emperor stood near the pathway, awaiting them.

Cadence and Rei didn't bother waiting until they were inside before sharing the details of what had been discovered. They delivered the information as the four of them headed briskly inside the dew-covered stone walls.

"I can't say that it is worse than I thought," Arasi said, "but the timing is far more critical. We're going to need to work in sync for this with unmatched urgency."

"We'll need to gather the other leaders of Mora," Cadence said. "Getting them to understand and accept what is happening and needs to happen is paramount. Unity Hall of Mora would be the most secure spot; the area hasn't felt the impact of the shifts. That is, if Emperor Ki-tae agrees that it would be safe to travel that far. I'm just concerned that anything closer to this area may put leaders in jeopardy."

"I agree, darling." The emperor nodded, looking closer to his age than he had a few days prior. "The land shifts are hitting Sentan and every land to the east of the Brin River brutally. With the most recent sinkhole near Mora Tanis, there is no way we could ask leaders to gather anywhere near the unstable land. Calon is farthest, but safest, at this time." He flashed a quick grin at Arasi. "I'll need your talents, and a messenger or two. So make plans as well."

"Without doubt." Arasi inclined his head, but his face was unusually grim. "No point in being anxious about it now though—clouds the thinking, and we need some clarity this morning," he declared, suddenly brightening up. "Now, why don't the both of you go and grab some sleep," Arasi ordered, ushering them out. "Preferably in one bed to save time of course," he called after them. To each other's relief, neither Cadence nor Rei acknowledged it.

*
**

As the sky was brightening the next morning, Cadence and her guards packed their horses to hasten back to Calon. Rei met them at the stable, where he, too, was packing to leave. "Where are you going?" Cadence asked.

"Back to Satura," he told her. "We can't be certain that the Ona estate is safe, since the mines are surrounding it, tunneling below the grounds. Arasi had some concerns, and I don't disagree."

"You're going to bring Mika and your family here."

"If she will come," Rei said. "Her children are safe at university, but Regi was going back out to survey other properties they've had reports on, and Mika doesn't want to join him. I'd like to convince her to stay here a bit, maybe under the guise of nanny for Kubo while we are away." He grinned. "Be careful traveling back. Regi noted that some of the land along the way was starting to crumble and made it difficult for the horses to get through. They were getting spooked quite a bit. They can sense the quakes before they happen, so pay attention."

"Thank you. Who knows how quickly things will deteriorate along our paths now. Sometimes I think having the details is worse. Ignorance makes one believe they are safe, even when they aren't." She stared at Rei with more to say, but the words dropped from her tongue. Instead, she held out her hand. "Get Mika, and keep Arasi out of trouble. Probably keep an eye on Ki-tae as well. I don't entirely trust either of them to take care of their own safety. That goes for you too. Please be careful, Rei."

Rei took off his gloves and entwined his fingers with hers. "You as well. It's not like we won't cross paths again if the world splits, we'll just have to swim across the divide."

"I can't swim more than a few feet." Cadence shook her head and laughed.

"A bridge, then!" Rei played ever optimistic, but perhaps they really had been too late in their admittance, however subtle it was. Reluctantly, he released her hand and stepped back.

Cadence smiled, then mounted her horse and waved her guards on. "Promise?" she asked. Rei looked up at her quizzically. "Promise we'll see each other again, no matter," she said. It was narrowly bold of her, but she thought that if the world was to split, she may as well at least say something, vague as it may be. Arasi would be somewhat pleased to know the walls they had built were wearing away. "It would break my heart to not see that purple-haired head of yours again." She glanced away and then smiled back at him.

Rei felt his own heart jump and followed her subtle flirtation. He peeked up at her, smiling. "Well, I can't be breaking your heart now, can I? I promise, Cadence, we'll see each other again." Rei bowed and then patted her horse's flank. "Be safe!" Then he turned to his own mount, facing away from Cadence so that she wouldn't see the pink hue crossing his face.

"Everything alright?" Kubo asked, coming up to the stables a moment later with the rest of Rei's supplies. Rei's face was still flushed, and he looked simultaneously happy and sad.

"Very much yes and very much no." Rei grinned to the confused apprentice. "Keep Arasi in check. I'll be back as soon as I can."

Chapter Ten

The council of Calon was currently overseen by Emperor Jiyan Allis. Though the council and the royal court worked together on all matters, the emperor maintained sovereign verdict. Jiyan had proven a calm and thoughtful ruler, often deferring to his well-trusted advisors and the council voice of majority. It was he and Cadence who had initiated the Mora Unity Pact that bound the sovereignties together in peace. Emperor Jiyan took matters about the imminent destruction and disruption to their lives in all seriousness and requested that every ruler of Mora and their advisors attend the summit in Calon.

It took weeks for the intended audience to arrive. The queen and king of Mora Avi, Calon's small mountainous neighbor to the north, arrived first. As Avi was set far from the other countries, they were shocked to discover the impact the quakes had been having. The king and queen of Firtan and the queen of Poltan arrived together, as expected. It was their respective countries that would be most impacted by what was happening, and their anxiousness was palpable. Emperor Ki-tae arrived shortly after the others but surprisingly not with Binder Arasi at his side.

The summit was scheduled to open with a large dinner inside Unity Hall, followed by a discrete initial meeting among the leaders and their advisors only. Formality and calm before the real work began. As expected of her, Cadence had traded in her customary military wear for something more formal: a gown of peach satin and lace. She wore her hair half up, the rest in waves along her back. No trace of trail grime or rough leather jerkin. She exuded radiance, and heads turned as she walked by on the way to the main hall. In the welcome lounge, a familiar face approached her with open arms.

Emperor Ki-tae's black silk robes were only a degree less radiant than his smile. After not hearing back from the Sentan emissary until the last moment, Cadence was relieved he had arrived safely.

"Arasi?" She hadn't heard from him, nor Rei, since she left the keep and had been worried.

"The roads have been treacherous, but within the borders have been stable. Arasi was traveling with me, but I asked him to assist a village we came across near Mora Tanis; his restoration skills were needed to make up for the crops lost. He is a little ways behind me but will be here soon. I promise."

The Sentan emperor smiled at her warmly, and Cadence thought she would blush at the look in his deep-brown eyes. He held his hands up and asked, "May I touch your hair?" Cadence nodded, and he removed one of the decorative white flowers he'd braided into his own long hair.

"An appropriate gift." He grinned as he fixed it into hers with a touch as gentle as a parent. He kissed her cheek. "You look like love," he told her. "Save a dance for me during the dinner, please." He paused, then added, "Since an emperor deserves an equal dance partner." Cadence bowed and returned his sly smile as he entered the hall.

Binder Arasi arrived as the dinner inside the hall commenced. Cadence kissed him as she greeted him at the entrance and embraced him for a long time, relieved that he was well.

"Don't tear up. You aren't used to wearing makeup; it will streak your lovely cheeks." He held her face in his hands and wiped her tears away. "We've missed you dearly." Arasi read the unspoken question on her lips and smiled. "We came across a slight issue on the road outside the walls. Rei was helping clean up and so might not make it here for tonight but should be here to grant you all the hugs tomorrow. Or more?" Arasi teased.

Cadence swatted him away and wiped her eyes. "You're more my family than anyone here, so I worry."

Arasi took her hands in his. "Are you coming in?"

Taking a deep breath, Cadence stared through the doorway. "In a bit." Her eyes darted to the full tables beyond the door. "I don't like crowds. I don't like being squeezed into things."

"Like that dress?" he teased, trying to lighten her mood.

"At least I dressed the part." She tugged on his frayed robes. "You really should invest in some updated garments," she quipped. "Once everyone is in the throes of their meal, I'll take my seat. I'd rather enter with as little pomp as necessary."

Arasi nodded. He understood the pressure and anxiousness the Calon walls created in his dear friend and wished he had a spell to relieve it from her heart. "You always do well, always play your part perfectly. Besides, it is only for now." He kissed her hand and headed into the hall with a flounce of his robes.

As the sovereigns and their guests, advisors, and family filled the hall, the musicians played a soft, calming melody. A few lesser diplomats were chatting, and courtiers milled on the steps outside, sighing over the various fashions from across the continent and whispering about what was happening. The atmosphere belied the chaos happening elsewhere. Cadence stepped away from them to the terrace on the side, overlooking the gardens she had happily played in as a child.

Cadence let out a deep breath and leaned out over the mezzanine. The moonflowers and night gladiolas were beginning to awaken, and she smiled. Being inside the castle grounds always gave her the sense of being trapped; out in the open, she could claim a semblance of breathing room. The warm breeze swayed the treetops against the darkening sky. The twilight in her homeland was always one of Cadence's favorite things—the stars peeking, the night birds singing. She stared up at the purple and pink ribbons of clouds above, lost in the sight of it. Behind her, another was lost in the sight of her.

Rei stopped on the steps, staring at the beauty before him. The sight of her took his breath away. Rei had never seen her so formal. She was more beautiful than he remembered, and suddenly, he felt sickeningly inadequate. Rei climbed the steps quietly and stood against the wall of the building with his hands behind his back, catching his breath and courage as nonchalantly as possible. "So, do we go inside, or do we need to wait to be announced? I'm not sure how this works."

Cadence spun around, and a relieved smile spread across her face. She didn't say anything at first, only walked calmly up to him. "Arasi said that you aren't fond of large gatherings, and I understand, but the lateness is still rude," she teased, then hugged him.

Rei was pleasantly surprised and relieved by her reaction. He held her tightly, burying his face in the side of her neck where the hair was pulled back and her skin was warm. She smelled like bliss, and he didn't want to ever let go. With little desire to do so, they parted.

"You finally cut your hair!" Cadence pursed her lips. "Hmm. I think the long hair suits you, but you're handsome regardless."

"You look…" Rei began.

"I know, I know. Very fancy and sparkly. Dresses aren't my standard wardrobe, but they're a fun change once in a while. Though, it is a lot of satin on this one, or whatever material this is." Cadence nervously smoothed the fabric at her waist. "It doesn't quite look like me." She grimaced down at her jeweled sleeves and shrugged. She absently touched the flower the emperor had placed in her hair. "I'm sorry, I—"

"Sorry?" Rei touched her chin, the first time he'd done something so intimate, and lifted her face up, all hesitation disappearing at the sensation of her against his hands. The look in her eyes granted him a confidence he hadn't experienced in years. "I love it. You're always beautiful. This is a different version of you, is all. Like putting a painting in a frame—it doesn't change anything, just adds to the beauty." His voice was soft, but his smile was as bright as starlight, his eyes dancing over her. "I like your flower," he told her, and Cadence reached up to take it from her hair. "That's a Sentan orchid."

"Emperor Ki-tae placed it," she told Rei, holding it in her hand and inspecting the delicate white blossoms closer. "It was sweet of him."

Rei chuckled. "Sweet, indeed. The white orchid symbolizes waiting for a lover to return," he told her. Rei knew that legend was something his emperor would have been well aware of. "The story is that when the petals turn orange, the wearer's love is nearby. It happens naturally after the bud has been picked for a few days, but…" Using a simple caster spell, Rei gently blew on the petals.

Cadence watched them slowly change color. Her heart began to beat faster as the flower turned the hue of fire. She kept her eyes cast down at the flower, something close to fear preventing her from looking up to meet his.

Rei took the flower from her hand and gently placed the newly orange orchid back in her hair. Then, once more lifted her face to meet his stare. Cadence was tortuously aware of his fingertips softly gliding from her chin and along her jaw to her neck, pulling her ever so delicately closer to him.

"I don't want to wait anymore," Rei whispered against her cheek. She closed her eyes and nodded, waiting for the lips she'd dreamed of for years to once and for all touch hers.

When she wrapped her arms around his neck and let him pull her close, time stopped. No night birds, no wind, no sound of guests chattering in the feast hall, no music. Two heartbeats, two breaths.

All he was aware of were her lips on his and her fingers pulling him closer. She tasted sweeter than the plum wine, and Rei drank it all in. After a brief eternity, they broke apart, slight smiles on both of their faces.

"That took far too long to happen," he whispered, rubbing his nose against hers. Cadence simply nodded and pulled him back to her.

They kissed again, more ardently, but soon became aware of the lingering glances from guards and late-arriving guests that passed them by.

Cadence pulled away and took Rei's hand in hers, leading him off the terrace and down into the lantern-lined garden below. "I suppose we shouldn't stray too far from the garden lights," Cadence said.

"The dark doesn't concern me—night is where I am most at home," Rei responded, putting his arm around her waist and pulling her close as they walked.

"So I've heard." Cadence smiled, thinking back on her conversations with Mika. "I've always held that something about you is different at night."

"How so?"

"Well, you're like the stars," she explained. "The stars are above us during the day, too, you just can't discern them as well because they are hidden by the brightened sky. Then night comes and they are suddenly alive with sparkle, lighting the way. I think that's the same with you. During the day, a part of you hides—you're less comfortable and more restless. At night, under the stars, you find comfort. You shine brighter."

"So I only shine at night?" he teased. "A bit rude."

"I'm not falling for it," she said, poking his side. "Speaking of falling, I've painfully caught my ankle on this path in the past, so mind the torches for wayward roots."

They walked quietly a few yards and stopped at a clearing bordered by tall bushes of fragrant night blossoms and moon lilies.

"This spot is Baron's Hedge. This was a favorite dreaming nook for me when I was a child—one of my escapes." Cadence spread out her skirt and sat on the thick, soft grass, holding her hand out for Rei to join her. "I was thinking about how much you liked being outside at night as a child, so I thought you would appreciate this. The dark lets you see the stars better, though I wish we'd grabbed a lantern at least."

Rei lay on his side and pulled her down next to him. He ran his fingers along her lips before kissing her softly and smiling. He held his hand upward. "The stars will share their light with you if you ask nicely." He stretched out his fingers, and it seemed as though the stars began to fall from the sky to give him their lights. In an instant, his hand held a softly glowing orb, which he then placed in the air above them, suspended by only magic. Cadence stared at the sky. The stars still shone above them, simply dimmer somehow.

"How did you…" Her words hung. Arasi had thought Rei didn't comprehend the extent or origin of his powers. Cadence was stunned. "You've always known."

"Known to do tricks? Yes."

"No. The stars. That's no trick." Her skin prickled at the energy buzzing around them and then softly settling, providing a comforting warmth. The orb above them twinkled softly, and it felt as though she was protected in a cozy blanket. "You know how powerful you are. No one should be able to do that to the stars."

Rei kissed her collarbone, and she shivered. "I am not doing anything. The stars and I have an understanding with one another. Nothing more."

"You're making light of it."

"Literally, I am." Rei grinned and swatted her nose. "Ssh, none of that matters now." He silenced her with a kiss, and they melted into one another's arms in the soft grass. Above them, the light glowed with an almost pleasant hum.

"Why did you wait?" Cadence softly asked.

Rei understood what she meant. It was a question he repeatedly asked himself. "Why did you?"

"I didn't want to be disappointed. Or hurt."

"I would never." Rei's eyes were tender as they stared into hers.

"I trust you, but life, not so much. If I admitted I loved you, the door to loss would open. But if I never admitted it, there would be nothing to lose, right? Regret isn't as painful as disappointment and loss."

Rei shook his head. "Because you don't say that you're in love, doesn't mean you aren't."

"Well, I didn't say it is an infallible theory." She laughed. "So, then, what is your reason? I did ask first."

"A variation of the same fallacy." He frowned. Rei's hand rested on her hip, and the temptation to wander was intense, but this wasn't the time or place, as romantic a spot as it was. Instead, he rolled onto his back, and Cadence snuggled under his arm. Rei reached up and tapped the glowing orb above them, and it silently exploded into a thousand beams of light retaking their place in the sky.

They lay in the darkness together, staring up at the stars until Cadence tapped his chin. It was a peaceful capture in time.

"We need to go back." The disappointment was heavy in her words. She sat up and stretched. "I'm certain we're missed, and dinner will be done before we get back if we don't go now. Aren't you hungry?"

Rei grinned. "Starving," he said, sitting up and sliding an arm around her waist. He pulled her into another deep kiss against him, attempting to make up for lost time. Cadence had behaved exceptionally proper, but her resilience was buckling. She threaded her hands into Rei's hair and pulled him against her. She decided then that looking up at him was her favorite view.

"Lady Cadence! Your Highness!" a high-pitched voice called out from the terrace, waking them from their reverie. "The emperor has been seeking you. He is familiar with your trick of hiding in the garden to avoid gatherings. Please, do not make me fetch you. My knees are too old for carrying."

"Yes, Chamberlain!" Cadence yelled toward the balcony. "We will be arriving shortly." They could see the silhouette of the elderly official raise his arm and nod.

"Lady Highness?" Rei stared at her, and she grimaced as she attempted to fix her dress.

"I'm sorry, I…"

"Like you, I'm not naive, and I am decently intuitive. Sometimes." He winked. "In line as the proper Calon regent, Arasi somewhat explained."

Cadence was relieved at Rei's reaction. "Technically yes, but also no. I'll explain later, after this bedlam of a dinner is done. I am sorry though…"

"Stop." With a firm grasp, Rei pulled her back onto his lap and stared into her eyes. "That's the third time you've apologized to me in a matter of minutes, for things you need not. Please, don't." He kissed her forehead lovingly and swatted her nose. "No need to apologize."

"I'm…" Cadence paused and sat quiet for a moment, snuggled against him. She took a deep breath and concentrated on his heartbeat beneath her fingertips. His presence was both exciting and calming to her. "I'm not comfortable when I am within these walls. It does something to me." She stood and offered her hand to him. "I am not myself when I am here."

"I understand." In his free hand, Rei produced a small orb of soft green light to guide their way. "You did promise to tell me about yourself when I made it here. So once these formalities are finished, I'd like that."

They entered the hall while festivities were in full swing, appearing only a touch disheveled and flushed. As they took their seats, at opposite ends of the hall, Arasi and Ki-tae exchanged mischievous glances and stared at the two of them and then back at each other.

"About time." The emperor poked Arasi in the side.

"Indeed," Arasi agreed. "Are those grass stains?"

Rei ignored him and sat down to eat as much as he could before they were whisked away for the post-dinner formalities.

While the downstairs of Unity Hall formed the rotunda for feasts and official sovereign debates, the stairs curving to the back of the building held the guest apartments and more modest, private meeting chambers. The sovereigns and their advisors, having eaten their fill, made their way upstairs as the night ended. Emperor Jiyan had seen to it that the finest of wines and cakes were laid out in the room, more in hopes of keeping moods light than as a kindness.

Rei sat on one of the cushioned benches near the door. Each sovereign was permitted to have one advisor accompany them, which is where Arasi and Cadence were. He preferred it that way. After traveling the last few weeks, Rei took advantage of the quiet to rest his eyes and think about what may come later in the night. The quiet was short lived, however, as the discussions from inside the room grew heated and loud only moments after the door had shut.

Though they weren't to begin discussions on the land shift event, the conversation soon escalated to that matter. Although the countries of Mora hadn't been in direct conflict for decades, there were always some underlying tensions. Cadence likened it to one of her country's lakes, saying "On the surface, peace, but beneath the waters are still big fish and little ones fighting for territory. That will always be a part of nature."

The leaders of Firtan and Poltan, the countries most impacted by the disaster, asked for privacy, and so the remaining leaders stepped out into the vestibule to wait. Emperor Jiyan sent for tea, and everyone made themselves as comfortable as possible on the benches lining the walls. Cadence sat on the same bench as Rei, a respectable distance between them, and put her head down onto her knees.

As the already late hour dragged on, Emperor Jiyan decided there was no point in staying awake to learn an outcome they would hear an earful of tomorrow. He offered apologies and suggested they reconvene for their official gathering the next afternoon.

Cadence and Rei slowly rose, stretched, and waited as Arasi and Ki-tae stoically bid each other goodnight before heading to their respective quarters in opposite directions of the hall.

"I'm hungry. Are you hungry?" Cadence asked Rei, when they were the only two left in the vestibule.

Rei shook his head. "Not overly, maybe thirsty, but I need to find my quarters…" Before he could finish, a stir down the hall caught their attention as they witnessed Emperor Ki-tae pass by them, in the direction of Arasi's quarters, complaining in Sentan about the druid playing hard to get.

Rei stared down the hall. "Mmm. Pretty sure I was with Arasi, but I guess he already has a roommate."

Cadence smirked and took his hand. "Well, come with me on an adventure, then, and I might find you a bed. Possibly a place to sleep as well." She led Rei down the stairs and out the main entrance way of Unity Hall, where servants were cleaning and already beginning to set up for the next day's session. She didn't say a word as they made their way across the courtyard toward the castle.

"Certainly are a lot of people still around." Rei could tell from the alignments of the stars that it was near to midnight or just after, yet servants and guards still hustled about.

"That's Calon efficiency," she told him. "Much of the work is done at night so as not to impede any of the day's events. Cleaning, cooking, stocking, guard training—there are quite a few things consigned to the evening." Cadence tugged his hand. "I thought you liked the night best, anyway?"

"I do, but not for work. For rejuvenation. And… other things."

"Oh? Other things, eh? So you only do 'other things' at night, then?" she teased, glancing back over her shoulder.

Rei came to a sudden stop and pulled her to him. "We can do 'other things' at any time you desire." He grinned down at her, his amber eyes sparkling as bright as the stars he'd stolen the light from.

"Is that so?" Cadence bit her lip, then led him off the pathway and around the side to a smaller cobblestone path leading up to a wooden door. The guard politely offered greetings and granted them entry.

"Be as quiet as possible," Cadence instructed. "Despite the hustle and bustle, most people are still sleeping in this part of the castle. Or worse, just woken and not in the best moods." Winding down a wide and well-lit hallway, she brought him into the master kitchen of the palace grounds where the night staff was already prepping for the morning. The objective of her mission, gathering something to eat since she'd missed most of dinner, was within reach.

Aside from the occasional smiles and nods, the porters and cooks paid them no mind and said not a word of protest as Cadence snatched up a small basket of fruits and pastries that were meant for the morning. It was amusingly obvious to Rei that she had done this before. Almost as quickly as they had raided the kitchen, they were back out into the hallway, and a few twists and turns later, they were inside Cadence's private apartments.

Once inside, Cadence and Rei let out relieved breaths.

"This has been an unnecessarily long day." She placed the basket on a table near the fire and turned to survey the room. "I think," Cadence said, taking a bite of a muffin, "that you should probably sleep here. The couches in the sitting room are shockingly comfortable. And"—Cadence decided to take a safe gamble—"my bed is also quite comfortable. Unless of course you desire to hear Ki-tae snoring all night." She walked over to the fireplace and added some logs to the dying embers, casting a warm, orange glow against the gray stone walls.

"Truly, truly a hard decision." Rei grinned. He walked up behind her and traced the loose strands of her hair with a feather-soft touch.

Cadence nestled back against his chest and then turned to kiss him. With no fear of interruptions this time, she ran her hands along his shoulders, removing his coat and shirt. Tracing her fingers over his bared military markings, she couldn't help but smirk up at him, remembering the first time she'd discovered them. Rei took her hands into his and kissed them.

"Let's see how comfortable your bed is."

"Oh, I think you'll be pleased," Cadence teased, pulling him into the bedchamber. As she playfully pushed him on top of her blankets, Rei drew her into his arms.

"Finally." His voice was husky as his fingers searched for the ties on the back of her dress. "Now, to get you out of this soft armor."

Cadence laughed as she straddled his lap. "Just tug harder. I won't mind if the ties rip in the essence of time."

Rei's muscles tensed as he deliberately tore the fabric with more eagerness than he'd intended. He lifted the dress over her head, freeing her from the hindering material. The thin under-gown beneath was sheer and did little to conceal her fullness. She nipped at his lips and grinned.

The sight of her body made Rei ache painfully for her. He lit a fiery trail from her lips down to her chest. "You are so very beautiful," he whispered against her skin, "and I have loved you for so very long."

Cadence pressed his head to her chest, burying her nose in his soft hair. She purred contentedly as Rei's hands kneaded her thighs, and the urgency between them began to build.

"What are you hesitating for?" She tugged on his hair. "It's night. Isn't this what you meant by 'other things?'" Cadence giggled.

Rei smiled and pulled her back onto the bed with him. "So very many other things," he said, pulling her down against his chest and threading his fingers into her long dark hair. "Whatever my Cadence desires."

Chapter Eleven

Morning bordered on noon by the time they awoke.

"You promised to tell me all about yourself once I was here," Rei reminded Cadence as they took their lunch privately on one of the Unity Hall's balconies before the events of the day started.

"Did you not learn enough last night?" Cadence teased.

"Last night was a decent start," he said, kissing her shoulder.

"It really was." She smiled. "Where should I begin?"

"Wherever you want, Lady Highness."

"Oh? Is that a hint?" She leaned back, choosing her words carefully. "I am not the leader here, I merely have the right to claim it if I choose. Imperial Sequence, they call it, and as such it can be required against my choice. So I'm still bound by certain formalities of the royal family."

Cadence peered out over the stone barrier at the people below.

Children were gathered at one corner of the yard, being entertained by a harlequin, and courtiers rushed to and fro among the servants readying for the additional guests.

"What I've always loved most about our country is the people. Many Calon citizens are born outside these borders, if you study our history; they are from all over the continent but came here and blossomed. We've so many cultures, foods, personalities. Though a shocking lack of delectable wine." Cadence glanced back at Rei, who was watching her intently. "In Sentan, the empirical family is seen as divine. Here, they are seen as sacrifices to the divinity that is the country itself. The Calon family crest bears the motto 'Service Until the Tomb.'"

She pointed across the courtyard to where white-capped mountains rose in the distance over the tree line. "I grew up, banished of sorts, to the city of Fellford, at the base of those mountains. I lived with my father's parents; Papa taught me mountain life, and Mama taught me to have fun. The town had so many wood-carved statues along the streets! My friends and I would climb on them, but that was nothing compared to the climbing we did in the mountains. It was a beautiful place to grow up." Cadence looked wistfully out across the sky. "Fellford was demolished by a landslide over a decade ago and became uninhabitable. My grandparents had already passed, thankfully, so they never saw the destruction of their home."

"And your parents?" Rei asked.

"My parents, Prince Erin and High Princess Cara, were…" Cadence hesitated, and Rei got the impression she was trying to find kinder words than she wanted to use. "They were busy and not so much the loving type. Children were a hindrance, and so they passed me off to someone else to deal with." Rei winced at the thought. While he and his mother had clashed, he never once doubted his parent's love for him. "Only the stars know where they are now. Presumed dead. Emperor Kaden was blunt that none of his children were worthy replacements for him, so they had no reason to linger here as bowing to the next in line.

"It was years later that I was plucked from home and placed in this castle, just as brusquely as that sounds. I thought I had done something wrong; no one had been aware beforehand that I was his successor. The sitting monarch makes their decision silently until such time as to begin the training for the progression of authority. I was miserable being taken from my family and put here with people I hardly knew as more than acquaintances, but my grandparents convinced me the decision was an honor. They were proud." Cadence shrugged. "I wanted to make them happy."

Rei understood.

"Of all the potential heirs, our sovereign thought my temperament best for the task at hand. I tried to think of it as my profession—a carpenter may love building bookshelves, but sometimes you must build tables to stay in business. I thought as long as I had my studies and lessons, I could accept the other parts of the mission. I thought that I was succeeding, but I was miserable.

"When I was about seventeen or so, the preceptor in charge of my progression decided on his own I needed what they called a 'cleansing of the will.' This meant they thought my attitude needed a physical reflection via freezing baths. I refused, and they attempted to force my submission, so I held him at knifepoint, and when they said I was mad, I decided I wasn't going to accept this anymore, so…" Cadence gave a wry smile.

"Emperor Kaden interceded. He told me that I had the right to kill the preceptor, but that it wouldn't change my course. Remember, I was property of the empire, not as disposable as the preceptor."

"You disposed of him?"

Cadence gave Rei a neutral look and shrugged. "Grandfather and I came to an agreement: If I completed infanteer training, I would earn my choice of paths, and he would select another heir. I succeeded, and he kept his word." Satisfaction beamed on her face at the memory. "So long as the new heir was obedient and I did my part to support them, I could choose my own life. Of course, we had some caveats, such as deferring to council permission on certain affairs, not disappearing off into the wilds and all that."

Pausing to fill their teacups, Cadence took a moment to finish the rest of the roll she'd been eating. "Baking was one of the passions I had; out of practice now, but back then I could make breads fluffier than this. But I convinced myself I needed something with less roots than a bakery or sweetshop. I ended up finding the path with the most freedom to take me away from here: Prime Mediator. I could oversee our strategic interests and travel far and wide in the name of diplomacy."

"Do you ever wonder what your path would have been like as empress?" Rei was curious if he knew the answer.

"At times like this? Yes!" She laughed. "But just because I want to get my way. Jiyan was better suited for this life than I was from the start—commanding in the calmest of ways. He's the penultimate loyal Calon."

"He's an admirable person," Rei noted. "I think you chose well."

Cadence sat back, gazing out across the courtyard. "Still, being within these walls makes me ill at ease. I am ever cognizant of protocol and expectations, of what is wanted of me. This place is a giant tomb, and I swear I breathe my last breaths every time I am here."

"Wildly melodramatic, wouldn't you say?" a deep voice beside them said. Cadence and Rei looked up to see Emperor Jiyan, in clothes as plain as the servants except for his circlet, standing at their table. "You feel such angst because you murdered that preceptor. Or not." He shrugged. "She has never given any of us confirmation. I believe it though. Pardon the intrusion, but we are gathering now," he informed them. "Please join us." Jiyan brushed Cadence's arm warmly, and she nodded.

Rei and Cadence stood, and for a moment, took in the view once more.

"Calon is a good home, just not in here," she explained. Rei leaned over the balcony, watching the puppet show below and at the giggling children entranced by the comical performance. "They're adorable." Cadence sighed. "If you're not of royal blood, the empire does well to protect its people, I will give Calon that, and my cousin has proved an amazing caretaker. The children here, all of the citizens, are loved."

"I've always admired Calon, and don't think I'm pandering." Rei smiled. "Treatment of certain ruling family members aside, the nation sets a good example."

"Calon is a fine portrait of Mora—not created from layers but instead a mosaic. I've always admired that, even when Mirin besieged us; they could have had a home if they'd been a bit more amicable." Rei nodded. Mora's battles with Mirin and the unrest it spawned had been his initiation into fighting during his early days with the regiments. "Calon is a great nation, but not so much a great home in my case."

Rei turned and wrapped his arms around her. "Perhaps, when this is done, you might like to make your home elsewhere."

Cadence adoringly met his eyes. "Is that so? Am I to move into your master's keep full-time?" She laughed.

He kissed her nose and then her lips. "Perhaps."

*
**

The Unity Hall of Mora, located inside the royal grounds of the Calon Emperor, was itself a castle; the crest of the Hall's domed roof overshadowed that of every building within the fortified stone walls. The meeting hall had been built two sovereigns ago, at the behest of the leaders of Mora, to have a neutral and safe meeting point. The great open hall, where the feast had been, took up most of the girth, while apartments for diplomatic guests and facilities lined the sides and floor above.

As noon came, leaders and their advisors from Mora gathered and settled into their seats inside. Long tables, set with water and fruits, had been placed along most of the rotunda in a horseshoe formation. Additional advisors and transcribers were permitted along the walls, and the large chamber appeared as crowded as it had the night before at dinner. Cadence and Rei entered together after most were already seated and went to their respective tables.

"Forgive me, but you both look terrible." Rei smirked as he took his seat behind Arasi and the emperor. Both seemed exhausted and already annoyed.

"We were up all night," Ki-tae explained. "Unfortunately." The Sentan emperor mock pouted at Arasi, who shrugged and rubbed his eyes. Ki-tae gave Rei a once over. "My darling, don't you look incredibly well rested for someone I assume didn't sleep much last night? Or, this morning?"

"I slept extremely well," Rei bragged, and was relieved when Emperor Jiyan called the group to order before anything more was said.

Chapter Twelve

Though each country on Mora had their own laws and cultures, nothing was more important to them than the peace of their united world; a lesson hard learned when they had to unite decades earlier against invaders from the island nation of Mirin. At the time, the Sentan had been the newest inhabitants on Mora, having come from a smaller continent to the south and taken the unoccupied rocky peninsula to the east. There were still pockets of distrust about their magically inclined new neighbors, and conflicts were not uncommon. Their defeat of the Mirin proved they worked better together, and they vowed to maintain that. The Mora Unity Pact solidified that vow. However, the upcoming disaster was adding an unseen stress. With a hundred miles of inhabited land about to be unlivable, where would the displaced go that wouldn't overwhelm the others?

After setting the stage of what was transpiring, Emperor Jiyan offered his assessment. "It is one thing to welcome a few dozen new citizens each year, but another to take in several thousand in scarcely a few months' time. Food and lodging, hygiene and health all needed to be taken into consideration. The breaking apart of the land has already caused a shortage of necessary supplies for many people. We are already beginning to contend with limited resources."

"More importantly," Queen Yarin, the voice of Poltan, interrupted, "our citizens of Poltan, along with their brethren of Firtan, are not willing to abandon our homes. In our conversation last night, we take umbrage at other countries telling us what is best for our own people."

King Oran of Firtan stood and declared his agreement beside her. "If the council is gathered to offer their assistance in what is best for all of us, then we demand another path be explored."

"Our time is limited, particularly yours." Jiyan was blunt with his words.

Queen Yarin narrowed her eyes at Emperor Jiyan and glared at the other leaders. "I'm certain that was not a threat, but it most assuredly sounded like one."

"Well, it is, just not from the people here," Emperor Ki-tae offered. "Nature, or whatever the cause of this disruption is, has its own timetable. No one here, not Calon or Poltan, not any of us, has a say."

"So the smaller nations should be allowed to be browbeaten by the empires?" King Oran asked.

"You're being preposterous." Queen Lupir of Mora Avi stood from her seat. "This impacts all of us, not just your moneyed countryside. No one is trying to threaten anyone. We are all trying to help. You are willfully standing in your own way, and it isn't just your pockets or your people who will suffer. Cast your egos aside and accept the truths." Mora Avi was the smallest of the nations, but Queen Lupir and her husband, King Eru, were never ones to back down.

"Perhaps Mora Avi should keep an eye on its borders going forward." Queen Yarin gave a sideways glance to Emperor Jiyan.

"Now who is pitching threats?" Queen Lupir challenged.

Emperor Ki-tae rubbed his face and held up his hands. "We're off to a dreadful start, aren't we, friends? And we are indeed friends, in case that has slipped anyone's mind. And what are a few innocent threats among friends?"

Both Binder Arasi and Rei internally flinched at his words.

"Oh, the leader of the conjurers speaks!" King Oran sneered. "Can your druids not wiggle their fingers and fix this for us?"

Ki-tae tempered his response with a smile. "Perhaps, in a small way, that is indeed what we can do. It carries greater risk than I am comfortable with, but it may be worth it to keep us from one another's throats." He'd been up all night with Arasi debating on how best to proceed. "As the dashing monarchs of Mora Tanis are aware, one of our druids, Binder Ki-Maris, had been surveying the land shifts throughout the continent for the last year," Ki-tae continued. "Culminating with the sinkholes around our treasured trade city. Binder Ki-Maris had been making progress but hasn't been heard from in some time and is presumed dead. He was, however, organized enough to keep his notes and journals on stable land, which our scholars have been studying."

"Yet you did not share this with us?" Queen Yarin was indignant.

"Keeping secrets at a time like this is dishonorable."

Emperor Ki-tae frowned and bowed to her. "They were not secrets, our queen, just not common knowledge. Without understanding the notes, they would trumpet into your ears as hasty words of panic. We wanted to be certain we were communicating truths and not rumors."

Queen Yarin did not appear pleased, but she couldn't argue with that logic. "So, what are the truths?"

"That the land is going to collapse into a valley that will fill with water from the northeast coast. It will flood for miles outward and take years for the land to be stable and inhabitable again. Mora Tanis will fall within those parameters completely."

The room fell silent for a moment, before erupting into worried chatter.

"You're guessing." King Oran of Firtan shrugged. "We disrupt our peoples and the whole continent over a guess?"

"Not a guess, my friends." Ki-tae shook his head. "These disruptions are not unlike what we had experienced in Sentasiev before coming here, with a very major exception."

"Which is?" King Oran demanded.

"Trying to be explained if you would kindly hold your patience," the Sentan emperor responded, his tone unbothered. "Which is that the cause of these quakes and shifts appear to not be natural and therefore may not be stopping anytime soon." He held up his hands before anyone interrupted. "Detail on what is causing them is unexplained as of yet. That was what Binder Ki-Maris was focusing on before we lost him. Whatever that was comes second to maintaining the lives of the citizens in its path."

"Agreed!" Emperor Jiyan stood. A few moments of rumbling lingered before the other monarchs nodded and voiced their agreement.

Queen Lupir of Avi spoke up. "What can possibly be done about this? Not every nation on Mora have the resources that Sentan and Calon do." The smallest of the countries, Avi, had the least amount of citizens but also the least amount of resources.

Jiyan faced her. "I trust Calon and Sentan will agree to lend our resources foremost. We have a tentative plan we want to share, and we believe it is the most practical." He motioned for Ki-tae to continue.

"Thank you, dear Jiyan, the Ever Calm. We cannot stop what is happening, but we can keep the area affected clear and safe. The Calon forces, with some of our druids and casters, can monitor the sides that will be splitting and work to keep the secondary shifts and flooding contained, to a degree. That might at least save some of the land." He took a breath and held it in thought for a moment. "We'll also need to monitor our coasts for any slides or great waves that may surge from the splitting. We can't bind the ocean, but we can offer some shielding if needed, and we can train adepts to assist us without much time. The spells are easy if you have the strength."

"Of course, the magic users save the day!" King Oran snapped, and a mumbling of endorsement rumbled in agreement with his remark.

"Did I miss the part where Calon stepped back?" Cadence spoke up without rising, her voice cutting through the chatter. "Whatever saves the day is fine by me. Calon, at least, is not one to turn away help to save pride. I'd rather people didn't die or lose their homes just because we're too proud to work with our ally that has a tactical edge."

King Oran, flustered, sat down.

Emperor Jiyan added, "Our forces can seal off the dangerous zones and make sure the people are at a safe distance. Once that is done, we would be able to fortify and build up any of the towns that would be deemed safe. However"—he turned to the respective monarchs of Firtan and Poltan—"your people need to vacate at once to the sides they wish to stay on and understand that they will be separated for months, at least, until everything settles. We can't guarantee the new river that forms, if one forms, won't be swollen with vortices and rambling tides for months after. It may not be readily traversable."

"We offer no guarantee of safety despite those measures," Ki-tae added. "We've heard all the arguments and plans. Nothing can be done to stop this, only prepare. The continent is going to pull apart. The best we can do is let the sundering happen and help in the healing. Once the terrain has settled, our druids will walk the lands, healing and warding. In time, that should make the newly formed areas more habitable in less time. Until then, the borders of Sentan, as always, will be open to whoever needs them."

"As will ours," Jiyan announced, and Queen Lupir also offered their small country as home.

The king of Poltan added, "We would rather not desert our homelands."

"There's no shame in finding a new home," Jiyan told them.

Done with listening, Cadence broke her silence. "If it is a matter of living somewhere else or not living at all, that is no choice at all." They heard soft rumbles from the others in the hall, but Jiyan and Ki-tae waited in silence for her to continue. "However, I do have reservations. Emperor Jiyan, and Emperor Ki-tae, for this to work, the Sentan druids and casters, as well as our allied companies, would need to be directly along the sundering line? Close to where you guess the split will be happening? To use their magic, they will need to be within sight, and to use our might, we would need to be within physical reach. That's a lot of people to put in harm's way over what we all know is, as King Oran said, a guess. Even an educated one." She paused and waited for her words to register.

"Additionally, the time and resources it would take to reinforce the nearby towns for an influx of residents is more consuming than just having those people emigrate for a few years elsewhere," Cadence continued. "Time is essential—the gash could come far sooner than we have estimated. The better plan is to evacuate as far outland as possible and wait for the dust to settle and then rebuild. If something more is causing this, an outside force, as some are insinuating"—she cast a glare at Emperor Ki-tae—"then, there may be benefit in abandoning the lands and working to find the cause. Otherwise, we risk that it doesn't stop and grows worse, impacting our entire continent."

"You heard the concerns. What works for us does not work for them." Jiyan bowed his head toward the leaders of Poltan and Firtan.

"Putting others in danger to save empty towns does not work for me. Binder Arasi?" The druid had been watching in silence with Rei from across the room. "While these events are taking place, do you believe the rest of the continent will be placid?" Cadence asked, but she already knew the answer.

"No. There will be aftershocks, tidal waves along the coastlines bordering the split, sinkholes, and other geographical disruptions across the continent. Not as seve—"

"Then, who will be protecting those people?" She cut him off, her question directed to Jiyan and Ki-tae. She was met with blank stares and silence, as not even those sovereigns had thought of that. "We need to approach this as an attack. Yes, the biggest battle will be centered on Firtan and Poltan, but we cannot concentrate all of our forces in only those locations. We already know that we cannot win this battle. Let this one happen, but protect the others—we can assess the damage and any restoration after. We are unnecessarily risking lives."

"I understand your concerns," Jiyan confidently told her, "but I respectfully disagree."

Cadence's eyes narrowed at him. "You disagree with me?" She uttered her words softly so that only Jiyan heard, but Arasi and Ki-tae could read her lips and, more importantly, her face.

"As do I." Ki-tae's voice sounded hesitant, but his tone was meant to be soothing, as though he were approaching a rabid dog.

"Explain," she demanded.

The leaders of the countries in question held up their hands simultaneously, and Queen Yarin cleared her throat. "If the sovereigns present agree, then, we do not need to debate this. Our people wish to stay as close—"

"At the risk of letting others be hurt? Killed?" Cadence demanded.

"Risk is always present, but I think this is the best option." Ki-tae still kept his voice calm and respectful. It didn't matter if the others heard him, only Cadence.

"The legacy of your people exists because you fled destruction," she reminded him, "and were accepted here. You didn't try to push back the damage or heal the lands. You fled and assessed the destruction later."

"We had no one to help us. We were alone then, without compatriots." He held out his hands and smiled, despite or in response to the daggers in Cadence's eyes.

The Sentan emperor had to admit it was kind of alluring and couldn't help throwing a guilty glance in Rei's direction. The caster kept his eyes fixed on Cadence, his face sober, which made him look close to imposing. His eyes flicked to Ki-tae's, and the emperor read the sign of 'let it go' on his face. He ignored it. "Firtan and Poltan, unlike my ancestral home, are not alone, and we will do what we can to leave them intact."

"Decided, then. We prepare. Let's review the maps to see what towns we can fortify and where to set up the trespass lines," Queen Yarin of Poltan stated, and the other sovereigns agreed.

Jiyan turned to Cadence and whispered, "Don't contest this, please." She glared at him, and then at Ki-tae as he approached her.

"We are the powers here, and it is up to us to lead the decision for the greater good even if it means upsetting our neighbors. What they want is a death wish, and you know it," she told the Sentan emperor. "It doesn't matter what they want."

"Doesn't it?" Emperor Jiyan cocked his head. "When our countries signed that pact, it wasn't to take care of ourselves, it was to take care of each other, even if we didn't agree. Can we close down the lands and banish people elsewhere? Yes. It will cause conflict and clashes, because people don't like being forced into a decision. Will it overburden our other nations? Yes. Can that burden become a disaster of its own? Without a doubt. However, it is the correct choice here."

"I wholly comprehend what you are trying to avoid," Cadence explained, "but what if the split is wider than expected and the towns we thought were safe are destroyed? Filled with people now dead under water or rubble? If we are so concentrated on what is happening only in this area, who is to help when the waves inundate our shores elsewhere and wipe out villages? If we are cleaning up Firtan and Poltan, who remains to lend a hand to Avi or us and our citizens? Our resources are not infinite."

"No decision is going to be the right one." Ki-tae sighed and bowed his head. "We can only act on what is right for the majority."

"I fundamentally disagree that this benefits the majority," she stated.

"If you contest this, you know what the council will ask of you," Jiyan reminded her.

"Oh!" Ki-tae grinned wildly. "Now, wouldn't that be interesting!"

Cadence flashed daggers at him again, but his grin widened. "Do not tempt me," she warned.

"I bet you'd be fun to spar with on the debate floor, though. Much more of an opponent than this one." He nodded at Jiyan, who grimaced.

"Quite rude. I'm fair."

"Fair doesn't mean fun," Ki-tae informed him, and even Cadence shrugged in agreement.

"Your druid conclave," she posed to Ki-tae, "what is their confidence that this can be safely contained? That the other towns will remain untouched and habitable?"

"Highly confident. Potentially over-inflated, I will admit, but they're seldom wrong." The emperor stepped closer and lowered his voice, not caring if the others took affront. "I agree with you, in my own view, but as stated, we need to take their people's needs into consideration as well as our risk of being overburdened. Sentan's borders will never close, but a sudden influx of new residents would be destructive. It's the same for you and little Avi. So while, yes, this is the right thing to do for them, it is the selfish and most preservationist thing to do for us."

Cadence stood stiffly, her eyes searching the ornately etched walls of the dome. "I won't contest it. I don't want the burden." She bitingly relented and drew herself up. "I'll take lead on the field and reinforcement plans for those of us not magically inclined. Gather the names of our ally military leaders and deliver a list to my planning room," she instructed Jiyan. "I also need our current troop delegations. Assign me your selection of staff and have that done before dinner as well. I want to meet with them tomorrow." Cadence moved to leave but turned to add one more thought. "In my own view, I don't like any of you right now."

"Except Rei," Ki-tae pointed out.

"Except Rei," Cadence granted, and walked out toward the main castle.

Chapter Thirteen

Cadence laid in the grass of Baron's Hedge, staring at the cloud-filled sky. Sharing it with Rei had spoiled it for her now; instead of peace, it made her miss his presence. She replayed the conversations with the other leaders in her head, forcing herself to accept the terms and trust what was unfolding. With a bark of a few words, she could be the one deciding fates, the one shouldering the burdens. Jiyan would likely not fight her on it, maybe even be relieved to accept it. She didn't want that though, not by any means.

Covering her eyes with her coat sleeve, Cadence tried to absorb the quiet around her. Unfortunately, even the Hedge, as isolated in the garden as it was, was not immune to the sounds of guards training in the distance or merchants squabbling with shopkeepers just inside the walls. It was only quiet in Calon if you weren't expecting silence.

Both Arasi and Mika had offered the seeds that Sentan could be her new home, but it wasn't a garden that could be freely planted. It was misleading to think she was awarded that level of freedom. Her fingers danced over the sheath of the dagger at her waist, desperately wishing to use it to cut her ties to Calon and disappear into the mountains of Sentan.

Cadence made the garden her solace the rest of the afternoon and let it foster her composure. It was well past dinner when she returned to her apartments. She hadn't eaten anything since lunch but hadn't the desire to stop by the kitchens. She was comforted when she opened the door and found Rei waiting for her with a tray of food.

"Thank you." Rei reached down and produced a large bottle of plum wine from under the table and presented it to her. "Thank you so much!" Cadence laughed.

"Compliments of Mika," Rei told her. "She grew quite fond of you." He poured the wine into a glass for her instead of handing her the bottle, as she asked. "I knew the flavor would grow on you."

"What can I say? I guess I like Satura-grown treats."

Rei laughed. He was relieved that he was able to provide her some semblance of comfort. They sat quietly, staring into the fire, similar to when they had visited Satura together months earlier.

"You're leaving in the morning," Cadence said, after she had eaten. "Arasi said the druid conclave would be gathering volunteers with magical abilities, even those potentials from other nations. Do you know what the plan is?"

It was less of a plan and more of an idea, but it wasn't complicated. "We have to assess their abilities and hope they are at least talented enough to memorize a handful of defensive spells."

"That sounds ambitious given our timeframe." She poured the rest of the wine into her glass but didn't drink it.

"Simple. Everyone needs to understand how to harness and protect. The technique is called Rope and Shield training and is one of the first things young casters learn. Rope is pulling something toward you, Shield is pushing something from you. A simple, basic spell," Rei explained. She eyed him for a moment with a smirk. "What?"

"Of course it is simple to you. You have an innate ability for these things, so you don't see the difficulty for others." She brought her glass to her lips, finishing the sweet liquid. "Chances are these are going to be people who aren't used to working under such pressure while learning something new. For those who show promise, it's like sending new swimmers to dive with sharks."

"No it isn't, but I'm not going to disagree with you." Cadence took in his words and blinked in confusion, but Rei smiled. "I saw your face earlier, and I value my life," he teased. "But if that turns out to be the case, then we focus on getting that lesson through first before they are placed within danger's reach. It's the only thing anyone needs to learn how to do. In the easiest of terms, it is nothing more than using energy that each person already has and often exhibits without realizing it. Not quite a feat of strength."

"Impressive talk for someone with muscles."

Rei grinned. "You think? I always thought I was too… what was the word someone told me once? Wispy?" Cadence laughed, then suddenly her face turned melancholy. "What's wrong? I mean, aside from the world sundering presently on the agenda."

"We were so used to Mora being peaceful on the outside that we ignored what was happening inside. Signs were missed. Now we are rushing to fix something, and we don't even know how it got broken." Her gaze was thoughtful. "I understand there is more to Ki-tae's words on what is causing this. He believes in an outside cause, something man made, and Arasi is of a similar mind. We grew complacent in our comfort and missed things around us." She sat back and rubbed her eyes. "Maybe we couldn't have prevented this, but we would have had no need to be so rushed and our resources strained if we had been paying attention."

"Replaying this over and over in your head isn't healthy, and that's all you're doing now. Things were missed, and now we're aware. This is the next step in the staircase. Stay in place until we're ready for the next one."

"This plan may be the best we have, but it puts you and the others directly in harm's way while everyone else scatters into the distance."

"True. And that is something we understand when we take on these roles."

"Arasi and you, you're both dear to me, and essentially you will be standing right next to the split. Not much farther behind will be my troops, the people I've watched over and worked with for decades. Ki-tae will be safe, Jiyan will be safe; the rest of us will all be at the precipice."

"You won't be." Rei shook his head. "They wouldn't let you."

"In addition to Prime Mediator during peace, the position is also that of general during war, which this is. I will be serving beside the others— they would have little choice, and I would not allow it otherwise. I have duties here." Cadence paused. "Duties I do not necessarily approve of."

"Arasi, the emperor, none of us disagree in heart. The head is where the disconnect is."

"I know." She beamed and took his hand. "I'm trying not to waste time dwelling on what may or may not happen, but it's difficult." She stood and pulled him up with her. Cadence brushed the still-too-long hair from Rei's eyes and ran her nails softly along the side of his neck, causing Rei to take in a sharp breath and pull her against him to kiss her. "I'm so sorry," Cadence whispered.

"No more sorries, right?" Taking her face in his hands, he stared at her adoringly and kissed her forehead.

"But I am, this time."

"Why so, love?"

"For making you wait so long. I didn't realize our time would be limited." Her voice was solemn.

Rei arched his brow. "Oh? I didn't realize our time was limited. We aren't quite that old. I mean, the firelight adds wrinkles, but—"

Cadence laughed and kissed his lips to quiet him. "You know what I meant. This is why you make me at peace. We counter our worries together. We're both thinking the same thing, and we both know how foolish our thoughts are. Still…"

"We had our own struggles to overcome, and we succeeded. For the most part. That is hardly something to apologize for. You know full well I understand what you mean." Rei held her, stroking her hair and nuzzling her neck. "We are both sorry."

"You promised earlier to keep me safe. I don't require that. But I do require that you keep yourself safe."

Rei grimaced. "I just want everyone to be safe. I can promise that I will try to err on the side of caution. I won't be foolish. Possibly impulsive, but I'll be smart about it." He looked over to the fire and then back into her eyes. "I understand you can't promise the same."

Cadence nodded. "And this is why we were so hesitant before. Our timing is awful, isn't it? Now we've made a mess." She forced a laugh to hide the disillusion in her voice.

"Well, we haven't made a mess yet, tonight, have we?" he teased, biting her neck.

Cadence yelped and pushed at him, laughing. "Not yet." She tugged his hand. "Come to bed. We only have a few more hours left."

Chapter Fourteen

Rei, Urie, and Kubo finished their task as the last tendrils of daylight faded into purple around them. The three casters slowed their pace; the day had been peaceful, and there was no need to hasten into the lamplit keep. After returning from Calon, Binder Arasi had ordered them to reinforce each warding around the keep and town every evening.

"I know I shouldn't speak it—"

"Then, don't!" Kubo snapped, abruptly cutting off Urie.

"—but the last few weeks have been calm," he continued in spite. "It's been star still."

"I told you not to!" Kubo groaned. "All the work we've been doing has been for nothing! The keep is going to cave in tonight, for certain."

Rei stopped and turned the moment his foot touched the landing of the keep. "Star still. What does that even mean?"

"Unmoving, constant. How have you not heard that saying before?" Urie continued walking but stopped at the door. "What?"

"I have, and it irks me to no end with how inaccurate it is."

Urie crossed his arms and leaned against the door, directly over the handle, despite Kubo attempting to unlatch it. "How so, master of the stars? Are our tiny, glittering friends above not steadfast in their arrival and departure with each turn?"

"HA! See? Your own explanation counters it. 'Glittering.' Things that glitter are hardly still. It doesn't make sense at all." Rei's expression was pained.

"I'm genuinely perplexed." Urie motioned for him to continue, and Kubo turned to listen as well, since getting inside wasn't possible at that moment.

"Well, it's obvious you've never stood still yourself and observed them from a tranquil perspective. They not only glitter, they move, pulse. Much like our breathing."

"We can be still and breathing at the same time," Kubo piped up. "So you're both correct. Can we go inside now?"

Rei gave a hearty sigh and looked skyward for strength. As he followed the other two inside, Kubo fell back beside him.

"Master Rei, if you don't like the implications of star still, you can think of it in a different… light." She smiled, proud of the pun—proof she was spending too much time with Urie.

"How so?"

"I think it means dependable. Constantly dependable. I wouldn't say 'breathing,' that was a little weird, but yes, moving. Moving in a clear, dependable way. When one is star still, they are steady and true. Such as you."

Rei was taken aback by his young friend's insight. "Well, that is one way to consider it. Thank you, Kubo. Your words are very gracious."

"Less gracious, more so I know who to spend my charity on," she quipped.

Before Rei could respond, Kubo darted off ahead, passing Urie to be first into the kitchen.

*
**

At Arasi's insistence, they were up earlier than routine the next morning.

"It seems that Master Urie left in the middle of the night." Kubo yawned, still digging the sleep silt from her eyes. "He's left for something important already, hasn't he?" she asked Rei as they made their way to Arasi's study.

Barely awake himself, Rei grunted in acknowledgment and offered Kubo a bite of the flaxseed biscuit he was eating. She casually took the entire thing. "Arasi sent Urie to task working with the other druid assistants in gathering our volunteers to train. They're meeting up somewhere just east of Firtan."

"And my mission?" Kubo asked warily. "Or will I be sentenced to cleaning the cobwebs while everyone else is being important?"

"Do not underestimate the importance of a clean druid's keep." Rei patted her shoulder. "It's a skill many lack. Such as Urie."

"I accept that I am the lowest rank, but a small bit of dreadful or dangerous would help me cultivate my skills, wouldn't it?"

"And that is exactly why I have called you to me so early, novice." Binder Arasi stepped unexpectedly in front of them at his study door, as if he had planned it perfectly. "Master Rei, isn't that right?"

Rei swallowed his amusement and kept his tone grave. "So dreadful and dangerous that we don't even have time to joke."

Arasi walked up to Kubo and placed a hand on her shoulder. "I am sorry. I know you are nervous about what you may be delegated, but matters being as critical as they are—"

"I will take up whatever needs be." Kubo straightened her stance, head up high.

"Such a good, willing child." Arasi smiled, looking back at Rei. "Much more agreeable than you at that age and Urie currently."

"That's because she hasn't spent as much time around you as we have. Yet."

"True." Arasi nodded. "Rei and I will be leaving before the end of the week. Before then, I'll need you to gather supplies to fortify the keep and reinforce the wardings already in place. You'll be in charge while we're gone, which may be months."

"Is that all?" Kubo grimaced. "So it's governing the grounds, which is just advanced level cleaning." She wrinkled her nose at Rei.

"Uh huh. That's it," Arasi confirmed.

"Don't be too relieved," Rei told her. "You'll still need to make sure everything is guarded and the daily processes are completed."

"Which I do often already," Kubo reminded him.

Rei nodded. "Yes, but normally Urie assists."

"Well, Urie makes it look like he assists," Kubo retorted, and Rei could only shrug in agreement as they entered the study.

"Regardless, you'll be entirely solo on this for a long time," Arasi told his youngest adjunct. "Captain Devi and the personal guard will still be here, but

I want them focused on safeguarding the town. Rei's sister, Mika Ona, is our guest, and while she will be of great help, it is not her responsibility to serve us; as stated she is our guest, and you will need to see to her."

Arasi sat at his desk and looked up at Rei and Kubo. "You didn't bring breakfast?"

"Your cook isn't even awake yet," Kubo reminded him.

"See? Already failing at governing the place and I'm still here." Rei walked over to the window to hide his grin. The sun was just beginning to peek through the trees. Arasi let out a comically dramatic sigh. "We will still have citizens coming to the keep and requesting caster assistance, which you will need to make decisions on without compromising yourself. I don't foresee any problems, but you need to be prepared in case concerns arise. I don't want us to come back in four months and everyone has starved or dehydrated to death because the water became unfiltered or a rancid food spell was accidentally released. Between decaying food and decaying humans, the smell takes forever to air out."

"Oh, wasn't that what happened with the last druid, Jonne?" Rei solemnly asked.

"No, no. Before her. Jero, I believe," Arasi said. "Went away for six months, came back to this place turned into a crypt, only less lively. No one needs that many ghosts to deal with in one sitting. Incidents like that were what caused druids to start keeping less staff."

"This place?" Kubo nervously followed up. "As in here?"

"Oh, no, no." Rei shook his head and waved his hand. "This wing of the keep is a more recent addition, so not here exactly. But nearby."

"Yes, actually it was where the dorms and research libraries are now,"

Arasi elaborated.

Kubo's face paled, and it was all the other two could do to maintain the ruse. "Oh." She took a deep breath. "I'm going to get started on inventory. While we still have daylight." She left the room in her usual flurry.

"That was marginally cruel. Dead things and ghosts are about the only things that frighten her. You realize, we're going to come back and she's going to have been sleeping on the floor of this room the entire time." Rei laughed.

"Think she'll even be able to sleep?" Arasi asked, turning to survey the stacks of books and papers in the study. "I'm more concerned that she'll end up warding the place into another plane of existence. Although also very curious. Either way, it should prove amusing to see what we return to."

Shaking his head, Rei sat down at one of the tables as the druid rifled through his shelves. "Where do we even start with this?"

"We start at the bottom, with the simplest." Arasi pulled a book from a shelf and brought it over to the table. "We need our casters to push or pull. Keep landslides, floods, rifts, at a slow and manageable movement. The skilled users, the bulk of our druids and casters, we'll have at the fault. A select few, we'll send to the coastlines to manage units for the rushing tides we may encounter. They won't be able to stop a tidal wave, but they might perhaps lessen the impact, keep people safe. Basic momentum manipulation. Not hard."

"Not hard to us," Rei said, remembering what Cadence had told him. He skimmed the page in the book Arasi had brought over. "Tricky to learn for those not as skilled. We'll be surrounded by novices, and that is describing them kindly."

"That's why we'll make a few copies of this spell and add some notes to it. Those with less of a temperament for this line of work can refer to the paper. Practice on some seashells or whatnot."

Rei paused in thought for a moment. "Note not to practice on the tides. That's how accidental tidal waves happen."

"Truth. So, find some paper and ink. I'll find some wine and food. We have some writing to do."

"Nice that you volunteered us to handle the paperwork while the other druids get their hands dirty." His words weren't a complaint but Rei's own observation. "Something in that decision is more about the cause and not solely the destruction."

"Yes. Because whatever the cause is, we may end up needing to push or pull that away as well so we don't end up here again. From the notes that Ki-Maris left, it was evident he sensed something was underground, pushing through the continent. He likened it to the sensation and residual sounds of mining."

"Not a creature of some sort?" Rei asked. "Some, behemoth worm?" He'd said it in jest but for a moment thought it did make sense.

Arasi shook his head. "No. He was an earth binder and knew whatever it was wasn't natural. He was certain it was mechanical, and before you make assumptions, Ki-Maris was of the belief that it did not originate with Mora, but north of here."

"Almost like we happened to be in the way."

"Exactly. That's why the rulers stayed behind in Calon; Ki-tae is explaining the findings to them. He's making it clear we are not acting on this information now, that the focus is on taking care of our people, but we need to make it a priority after. There are already a number of far-fetched ideas being floated with the paranoia and rumors already spreading. We can't divide our attention." He paused for a breath. "Now. Sustenance for our long day!"

By the time the druid returned half an hour later, Rei had already completed almost a half dozen copies. "How many more do you believe are needed?" he asked.

"Conservatively, I'd say 100." Arasi poured a glass and handed it to Rei, who stared at him. "I'm being serious."

"Then, start writing." Rei smirked. "I'm not going to be the only one suffering hand cramps from this."

Arasi laughed and took a paper and ink jar. After a few moments, he rubbed his eyes, then stood up and retrieved a small, enchanted music box to fill the air. "Not distracting, is it?" he asked Rei.

"Not at all." It was common for the druid to use the soothing sounds when he had to work long hours of redundancy.

"Not as distracting as Cadence?" Arasi smiled, staring at him from across the table.

Rei didn't bring his eyes up from his paper. "Stop." Arasi put the quill down and folded his hands, looking at Rei intently until his senior-adjunct glanced up. "She's not a distraction."

"No, not normally," Arasi said. "However, things have changed. In several ways. Which I am extremely happy about." The druid's eyes lit up, and his smile beamed. "All the waiting and whining has come to fruition!" Arasi sighed. "It was heartwarming to watch the two of you together in Calon, however short that was. You both deserve that, and I am quite happy to see two who I love so dearly finally come together. Liter—"

"Don't!" Rei warned, pointing a finger at the druid.

Arasi laughed. "Fine. But, distraction, I meant that." His tone became solemn. "What we are planning on doing is perilous. More so for some of us than others. Cadence is going to be right alongside, sharing our peril. Urie will be at her side, as well as some of our best casters, but you cannot be."

Rei nodded. "I understand."

"Yes, well, understanding orders and following them are two different things." Arasi took a few gulps of wine and sighed. "Where her command sits will be pushed back from the rift. We, on the other hand, will be entrenched. We'll need to be fully focused."

"Do you believe I wouldn't be?" Rei was offended.

Arasi stared at him blankly. "Would I be harassing you to take up druid training if I thought you wouldn't be?" He rolled his eyes. "How is one able to be both very pleasant and very disagreeable at the same time?"

"I'm gifted." Rei shrugged, his pride still stinging.

"Remarkably so. You managed to win over the girl no one else could." Arasi smiled.

"Woman, not a girl. And I didn't win her, she isn't some medal or—"

"Yes." Arasi leaned across the table. "But see, you're distracted already. Jumping to Cadence's defense when she hasn't even been attacked."

Rei shook his head. "Arasi—"

"The goal is to complete our tasks, heal our world, and go on with our merry lives. A life that includes you running off with Cadence and then returning here to finish your commitment to me. Please keep that at the forefront of your highly focused brain. Thank you." Arasi sat back and took another sheet of paper. "I don't want you worrying so much about Cadence that you end up endangering yourself. Or her because you think she needs protecting."

"I would never."

"We both know a lie when we hear it or say it, because I have been in the same position a multitude of times and chose poorly."

Rei leaned back in his chair, arms folded across his chest. "I sense this is less about Cadence and I and more about you—" Arasi waved his palm to silence him, and Rei shrugged. "You believe in me enough to station me at your side constantly. This sudden lack of trust is insulting and assuredly comes from somewhere else." Rei lowered his arms and pulled his chair back into the table, while Arasi ignored him. Rei sensed the tumultuous thoughts bouncing around the druid's head and decided to ease back. He pulled a stack of paper and a fresh inkwell toward him. "My focus will be on our tasks, our immediate surroundings. In all these years I've not once disobeyed nor let you down. It would be loathsome to start now."

"With confidence, I can say that switching the positions, Cadence would not risk our mission for you." He grimaced. "I think." Arasi let out a loud sigh. "My mood has been filled with worry. For you, for Cadence, Urie. Even Kubo dehydrating away from fear of non-existent ghosts now. Fright over the wellbeing of our dear emperor, whom I had to positively bully into staying at the palace."

"It's a lot of worry to bear," Rei agreed. "An extraordinary burden for someone of your advanced age, I'm certain."

Arasi smiled at the mock insult. "I worry for our loved ones and for our people. Our lands are splitting by an unnatural force. I fear it is a dark omen of a change in our world."

Rei put his quill down. "I've felt it too, whatever it is. It's not organic and not born of Mora. Do you sense this is malicious, then?"

"No. Events can be ominous without having ill intent. I've picked up on nothing specific, nothing tangible. Perhaps some of the sensitivity is residual fear from when our people were driven from their homes by a similarly shifting world. Families and friends separated, scavenging for safety. Separation breeds contempt, and with that animosity."

Arasi's tone became solemn. "I was with the first group of offspring born here, the first Sentan to be true children of Mora, just as beloved Ki-tae. We thought that would be the end of our differences with the other nations, but it scarcely made a mark. It took a common enemy to reconcile their trust. War does create a bond, doesn't it? Even if only temporarily. So, it has me reminiscing about it all and wondering how grand this divide will be."

"Then, we bridge the gap." Rei shrugged.

Arasi's solemn face broke into a slow smile. "Your confidence is as large as the universe at the most interesting of times. I think you spend so much time outside at night, looking up at the stars, because that's where your power comes from."

Rei laughed. "Power? A caster's power comes from birth and books." He went back to the paper and began writing again.

Arasi eyed him knowingly. "A druid's power comes from nature, the elements. The stars, always bright and twinkling, like you. People wish on them, ever optimistic, like you. They study them and draw lines to create constellations, essentially creating bridges. Maybe if you realize where your power comes from, you can focus for the lot of us."

"Oh, I see? Train me to be a druid so you can retire and leave all of this on my shoulders? Well, no thank you." Rei laughed and took a piece of bread from the tray. "Now, let's get these written out so we can have a real meal when we are done. Sooner than we realize, time will be up."

Arasi laughed to himself at Rei already providing him with orders and not realizing it. His training would be over before it formally began.

Chapter Fifteen

Despite their initial grumblings, the countries of Mora worked swiftly to bring their resources together. Much more of the citizenry agreed to caster training than anticipated, which surprised Emperor Ki-tae.

"The bedevilment we've endured over the years, and now everyone is quick to incorporate into our ranks." He'd traveled to the northern coasts specifically to observe their training. The emperor shook his head and frowned as Rei brought him out to one of the courtyards. "Are they at least talented, or will this just be a useless pretense?"

"Remarkably enough, we seem to have underestimated most of them. With further guidance, they might one day rival our own casters," Rei explained, with a hint of surprise in his voice.

"Is that sarcasm or sincerity? It's difficult to tell the difference with you sometimes."

"Sincerity," Rei replied, somewhat insulted. "Given the vastness of the universe, it makes sense that magical abilities are present in more than only our Sentan blood. Appears we have some raw talent out here. It's likely the ability has always been present, they were just never given a chance to awaken it or learn what their particular skill was. Some of our volunteers are quite adept. If they had the benefit of our academies, they could—"

"No." Ki-tae abruptly cut him off. "The academies are restricted to our own people."

"Are the people of Mora not also our own?" Rei's tone was respectful, even if his words were a challenge.

Emperor Ki-tae arched his eyebrow and stared up at the caster, amused that Rei would test him. "Do not let my relationship with your master make you so comfortable with me. You're not under royal employ yet."

Around them, the courtyard hummed with the energy being rendered by the instructors and volunteers. Vocal incantations were not needed for Sentan magic; the spells were formulated wholly in one's own mind and forced out through the strictest thought control. As a result, the training had an element of silence to it that derided the effort involved. The emperor turned and commanded Rei to follow him inside.

They had been utilizing the remnants of an old Firtan garrison for their training. It was set several yards from where the ocean met the sand and high enough up to give a wide and open view of any incoming surges. The tidal pools created on the shore provided ample practice for their volunteers to master the ebb and flow they would need.

Ki-tae led Rei to a private seating area that offered an uninterrupted view of the shoreline, but small and far enough in the corner of the garrison to offer as much privacy as possible. Ki-tae ordered one of his personal guards to obtain drinks for them, before settling into one of the old, worn-out chairs that had been left behind. They sat in silence until the guard returned with two mugs of something cold and only slightly bitter tasting.

Emperor Ki-tae's troubled energy dissipated, but Rei yet regretted his words. "I meant no disrespect, Your Majesty." He apologized as the emperor handed him a mug. Thankfully, it wasn't the questionable tasting wine Ki-tae was so fond of.

"I did not take it as such." Ki-tae waved him off. "My response is meant for our current environment and not indicative of how I may reply in the coming years. Perhaps. Yes, we are all one people here, but that doesn't change what we have experienced at the hands and hearts of our Mora brethren."

He stared at the younger man, reading him. "You aren't so young as to not have experienced their bias toward us, Rei. You remember moderate struggles, but with a few years more than you, I remember how unlimited that animosity once was. Forgiveness has been granted, but caution remains. Understand that is why I am not keen on the idea of simply throwing open our Academy gates to any who knock. We don't even do that for our own citizens. As an Academy graduate, you are aware of that." He paused to take a drink and sighed. "Just not yet. It isn't the right time. In full honesty, that time may be a long way off."

Rei nodded solemnly. "I thoroughly understand, Majesty."

"Now, if our Mora brethren want to set about opening their own academies of study, I would be happy to encourage them to do so and provide excellent resources. It would be an interesting training position for our casters and potential druids to assist as teachers." Ki-tae grinned brightly. "Oh, I do like that idea quite a bit! But"—he turned to Rei—"don't go mentioning that to anyone just yet. Once this travesty is laid to rest, we can revisit this discussion."

"Agreed." Rei smiled. "I think that would be an admirable direction to take, Majesty."

Ki-tae rubbed his hands together, as if anticipating a great secret. "Now, tell me. The talent you are seeing, how powerful? Those of a highly developed caster? Druid rank? Something beyond and yet unknown?"

"No." Rei shook his head. "All still at novice level. Most of them seem surprised by their talent for casting. If you examine the history of Firtan and Poltan, anything magical was always discouraged from a young age as being a practice rooted in deception. So even those who felt they might have had skills pushed it from their minds. Now encouraged to use it to save lives, they're opening up."

"Is there a chance that in itself is a deception?" Ki-tae asked. "That some within those ranks are highly adept but for the sake of remaining hidden act counter to that? Even if only for their own protection?"

Rei thought for a moment, surprised by the emperor's line of questioning. It hadn't occurred to him. "Undoubtedly there could be a chance of that. Though, it isn't something I have sensed with them. Even before, when I'd spent time in these lands, it's not something I had ever felt a perception of, let alone seen in action." In Calon, and the short time he was in Mora Avi, he'd seen no sign of other magic users, which was easy for an experienced caster to recognize. "Why are you asking? Have we discovered something?"

Emperor Ki-tae shook his head. "Merely a thought," he replied. "Just because this event seems to be ending at the apex of Firtan and Poltan, doesn't mean it didn't also begin here. There's potential that it might have been caused by magic gone unchecked, or an intentional spell."

"True. But the last identified magic user in the area, and currently unseen for some time now, was a Sentan: Binder Ki-Maris and his adjunct, Kurus."

"That is what prompted this line of thinking," Ki-tae explained. "Could it have been Ki-Maris, meddling with something he shouldn't have? Quite possible, though not probable. Or the possibility of someone else confronting him? Perhaps he stumbled across something he shouldn't have. Or someone. Magical accidents have been known to happen, that's why druids are assigned multiple adjuncts. Everyone always thinks it's to provide training, but really it's to keep our most powerful from being unchecked."

"Should that be close to the truth, I don't believe you'll find an unchecked magic user among the other countries," Rei offered. "Though in Sentan, among our population where magic is common enough to not turn a head? I wouldn't be shocked to find druid-level skills hiding under several cloaks."

"Now isn't that the voice of experience." Ki-tae winked. "But an excellent point. Perhaps we need to take a closer look at some of our own. We are not above being destructive, whether by mishap or intent."

The emperor sat back and yawned. "So much travel, it's exhausting. I've always preferred the comfort of being stationary, and the older I get, the more sullen it makes me to leave the contentment of home. When this is done, I don't think I'll leave the palace grounds for a few months, at least. Have you thought of your life post sundering?"

Rei was caught off guard by the rapid change in conversation. "As you said, this has been an exhausting experience, and I haven't given it much thought. Seems never ending, doesn't it." Ki-tae nodded. "But should it actually end, I'll head back to Binder Arasi's keep, I suppose? Picking up where I left off before this became our everyday life."

"And where did you leave off?"

Rei thought for a moment, unsure why the answer wasn't coming to him. Arasi was always busy and thus he, Urie, and Kubo were likewise busy. Try as he might, he couldn't remember the last venture that required his attention before the quakes took precedence. His brow furrowed in thought, but nothing came to him. "I don't know. It's been so long, I honestly can't remember."

"Sounds like the ideal chance to leave that behind and start on something new, then. No use picking up what you don't remember putting down."

Chapter Sisteen

Cadence scanned the horizon from the Calon base camp as she had done every morning for the last three months. She began each day by watching for breaks in the red-coated sands and hoping this would resolve soon. The waiting, which had put a stop on everyone's life, had become the worst part.

The Sentan casters had used a transcoloration spell along the area that was expected to split first and suffer the strongest of tearing. They had been able to get close enough to coat the beige ground a light crimson.

"Morbidly appropriate," Arasi, who was leading the magic users, had noted. "It is, after all, going to be a rending of the flesh of the earth." That had been two months ago, and Cadence hadn't seen him, nor Rei, since.

Quakes had started coming daily and lasting, leaving crevices in an almost orderly western path. The ground in the area crumbled making the task at hand more treacherous. The Calon regiments and those from the other countries had already been moved back twice.

"Hope you've been keeping up with your running drills," Cadence had informed her company. She'd only been half joking; with the swiftness that sinkholes and crevices appeared, jumping and dodging would be lifesaving. A few serious injuries had already been treated from unwary soldiers.

Their presence at the fault was twofold: The soldiers acted as guards, keeping the area free from any who would try to pass too close, which, not surprisingly, had already been a full-time task. Their forces constantly had to escort citizens back from the shops and farms located nearby, insisting that they had to return home for a few items. Several buildings on the outskirts of the trade city had already been shaken into rubble, but that didn't dissuade the residents from demanding entry. Reminding them that their lives were at risk more than their material goods did little to sway them.

It was also their order to act as reinforcements for the Sentan druids and casters when the ground did split—whether they would realistically be able to help was debatable. The soldiers were available to lend whatever physical assistance they were able, with the few casters among their ranks leading the way.

"This morning's shaking was worse than Kubo's snoring," Urie said, entering the post. Cadence was grateful he had been assigned with the druids on the Calon side of the fault. Binder Arasi had divided up the groups and, despite his prior conversation, decided not to put Cadence and Rei near one another, lest one of them ended up doing something stupid for the sake of the other. "I walked the perimeter. The rumbles are light but constant now, like walking on top of a raging river. My feet are still vibrating."

"It will be any time now," Cadence said. At this point, she just wanted it to be over. Once the dust settled, there would be so much still to do, and she had already started working on those logistics with Emperor Jiyan and the Calon council. She grimaced at the thought that no ending was in sight, at least for any foreseen time. "Lia and the girls are doing well at the palace?"

He nodded. "The emperor and empress made sure of it. I know they're safe. We heard from Kubo as well. She and Mika have been taking in some of the nearby townsfolk who've become uneasy. I'm glad they're all safe. Not so sure about us though." He laughed. "We might become earth food before the day is over." As opposed to what Arasi thought, the caster did indeed have a sense of humor, though it was more of a dark one. Cadence enjoyed spending her time with him.

"We haven't bathed in some time, so I'm sure we'd be spit back out," she offered. "We wouldn't be an appetizing flavor right now."

"This may sound odd, I'm sure, but I'm not terribly worried," Urie told her. "I think being on the precipice like this is thrilling."

Cadence shook her head. "It is obvious Arasi doesn't let you out much. Though, I can't say that I don't understand. When I was younger, more so than you are now, I was trapped behind the walls of Calon. It wasn't all that exciting. One of the reasons I joined the scout and ranger units was to have adventures, though not quite as intense as this."

"I'm not saying I enjoy this, but a purpose like this, it moves me."

"That's the quakes," she retorted. "Not everyone needs purpose, and not every purpose should be a thrill ride," Cadence told him.

Urie shrugged. "Agree, but when you live in the shadow of those with great purpose, you grow desperate for your own."

"Arasi's occupation in itself is purposeful, and trust me, that isn't always a thrill. That's why Arasi likes to seek other, more, uh, wanton adventures." She grinned, and Urie laughed.

"It's not only Arasi. I expect that from a druid. I have Rei to contend with as well."

"But Rei isn't your competition." Cadence was confused that Urie would consider him such.

"No, not competition. I mean, it's difficult since you're not a caster," he tried to explain. "I'm still at the stage where I am assigned my duties, with little time to make discoveries to call my own. My skills are used for caretaking, not creating, so I make no impact. That can be frustrating sometimes."

"I understand. Every family has competition. Imagine how Kubo must feel."

"Eh! Kubo is the youngest of the family—they are supposed to feel that way!" Urie laughed. "We all know she's wildly talented. Self-confidence needs to be worked on, though. So we poke at her. On purpose."

"Spoken exactly like an older brother!"

"Maybe, but don't—" Urie was interrupted by a low and long rumbling in the distance, akin to thunder but not quite. "Uh oh?" He stared at Cadence, and they sat in stiff silence. The dirt under their feet trembled, then stilled. "Nothing, perhaps?"

Cadence scanned the fault with her telescope. "Any time now, right?" She handed the scope to Urie, and he peered out. "Nothing seems to be further compromised, but steam is rising from some of the cracks. We're getting closer."

"If the rattling of the tent poles is any indication, a lot closer," Urie agreed.

During the last month, the ground had compromised so badly that even with guidelines, no one was able to cross the grounds if they didn't have wings, which meant no one. Binder Ki-Avia, stationed with Cadence and her company, had nearly fallen victim to the swallowing earth when she had first arrived. A flora binder, she had been able to manipulate a nearby root to stop her fall until Calon troops reached her with ropes, but it had been close. No one was permitted within several yards of where the transcoloration began now.

"Alert Arasi," Cadence said. "They might not see the same thing on their side, but this is a clear warning." Cadence gathered her personal supplies as Urie cast the communication spell. "Keep watch. I'm going to alert the other commanders and the rest of the company to be ready to move, and I want to see for myself what it looks like at the fault. Anything more happens, send up a flash and get out here."

Along the perimeter of the anticipated fault, guidelines had been staked. Since the ground wasn't to be trusted, the amount was doubled and reinforced by magic. It wasn't a guarantee of safety, just a precaution that was better than nothing. If the casters and soldiers got into trouble, at least they may be able to find their path away from the most dangerous area. Cadence tugged on the ropes, making sure they were still steady, still unmoved.

"I reinforced their hold spell this morning," Binder Rina said as she walked up next to her. "Must have been foresight."

"You anticipate it's time then too?"

Rina nodded. "Both too soon and yet not soon enough." She reached up and tied her long blond hair back securely into a bun. "I am confident what we have been waiting months for is now only moments away. If you're in agreement, I'm going to order our druids and casters to align."

"Of course." Cadence nodded. "We'll align behind you. At worst, we wait like we've been doing every day, and at best, we are ready to confront this."

"Truth be told, I hope it's the latter." Binder Rina sighed. "I'm sorry."

*
**

On the eastern side, the company consisting of Binder Arasi's most skilled magic users and the other half of the allied military forces and volunteers had felt the ground shake as well.

"The tremors are consistent, progressing with lightning speed," Arasi called out to those around him. "Urie sent a message from their side—it's the same situation over there, same jolting movements. The sundering is imminent."

Rei nodded in agreement. "I can tell that it is close now, right under us," he said quietly, so that only Arasi could hear him. He didn't want to put the others on edge. "There is a pull, like the tides, and it isn't conceding this time. Moving farther out, like a tidal wave." Over the last few weeks, from necessity and not from desire, Rei had given in more to the druidic powers he had always sensed were in him. The direness of the situation, along with comments from Arasi pricking his nerves, had granted him more acceptance of it, if only for the time being. Still, it was not something he wanted shared among the others.

The weeks building up to this had been the most stressful they had endured. Resources were limited, and perspectives were grim. For the Sentan casters and regiments, they had only old stories from their elders about seeing the ground split. At that time, the druids had nothing they could do to stop it, only save their families and flee to the rocky land to the north they only occasionally traded with. There had been no time for planning, no time to reflect on what leaving meant. Not everyone agreed to leave, not everyone who did made it. To Arasi and the others, who heard those stories from firsthand accounts, what was happening now felt like a chance at redemption, but it still weighed heavily on their strength.

"Remember to pace yourselves," Arasi reminded them as they cautiously moved out toward the plumes of steam breaking through the ground ahead of them. "This could last hours or days."

"Hopefully not." Binder Pollis shook her head. "In the middle of an active quake, one that may continue on for an endless time, we'd have no way to get supplies. Or rest. Even restoration druids such as us need to be able to collect our energies. Don't bring ill luck down on us." She looked back at the base camp, shrinking in the distance. "By the time we get to the crevice, we'll already be exhausted."

Arasi halted and followed her gaze back as well. "Binder Pollis, stop here with your casters. Use a declaration to tell the other binders to start coming out, but don't rush. Keep them steady."

"Prepare the waves." Pollis nodded. "That is a good plan. What about you? You should stay back as well, follow your own advice."

Arasi shook his head. "We're not getting up to the edge. Just a bit farther to get a head start. We won't move up to the crevice until you reach us."

Binder Pollis grimaced. "I'll join you. My casters will stay here in wait."

"We'll make do," Rei told her. "We don't want to exhaust ourselves too early. We'll stick with the shifts we planned." He paused. "Of course, that's only if all goes according to plan."

"What is wrong with the both of you? Stop saying such things!"

"At least not out loud," Arasi added with a smirk. "Plans often become nothing more than outlines when the actual adventure begins. Always plan to not follow the plan!"

Binder Pollis shook her head. "That doesn't even make sense."

"No, no. It does. Trust him," Rei told her, just as the ground began to tremble once more. "Brace yourselves!"

An earsplitting crack threw the three of them and their allies off balance as the dirt beneath them began to sift away. Arasi, Rei, and Pollis froze and stood awestruck as the ground a few yards ahead of them sundered and disappeared. "You cursed us!" Pollis glared at Rei.

The caster shrugged. "All in now, I guess?" He turned to Arasi, who nodded in confirmation.

A deep growl sounded from the ground beneath them as it started to shift and tremble. "All in. Now!" the druid ordered as Pollis sent up a flare for the others to follow. Well synchronized, the magic users and their physical backup converged. At a steady pace, the formations moved as one, their magic charging the air around them, giving the dust an ominous glow.

Chapter Seventeen

From his position on the other side of the divide, Urie's legs wobbled as the ground shook. Hardly a breath later, both he and Cadence saw the flares arc across the sky. "I changed my mind. I am not ready for this, but I have no choice now!" he shouted as he rushed to join the other druids in their ranks, almost leaving Cadence behind.

Cadence ordered them to advance, staying behind their line of magic users and within reach of the guidelines. With eyes fixed to the horizon, watching for any of their own flares they would need to respond to, the soldiers formed a sturdy wall of defense. The druids and their casters, most already advancing, had begun working with their energies to try and calm the crumbling grounds. Cadence felt the elemental forces radiating from them. It wasn't unlike being caught in a lightning cloud on the mountains when she was a child and similarly frightening.

In only seconds, the crumbling sounds around them grew and became raucous as the air turned opaque. Cadence could tell that something was wrong. As unexpected as everything already was, something more was brewing. She couldn't place it, only sense it, and it was more than just the caving ground.

Cadence called out again for everyone under her command to hold fast to their guidelines as the rumbling grew to a deafening roar. It wasn't just the ground splitting, it was the entirety of Mora breaking in two. *It's worse than we all thought*, Cadence thought as she was hit with a sharp pang of worry watching Urie take off running toward the fault with the other casters.

*
**

For what seemed like hours, the ground shook nonstop. Arasi's face contorted as he used his will to help lessen the destruction. Pressure and mist from the ocean surging up through the fault enveloped his legs as the land gave farther away.

Try as they may, the druids couldn't stop the damage but hoped to soften it by forcing it to happen slowly and controlled. They were the closest to the action, and the air was littered with steam and rocks, making breathing near impossible.

"I told you a mask would be a good idea," a muffled voice said from beside him. Arasi glared at the bit of purple breaking through the dust cloud.

"You look stupid." Arasi coughed.

"Yes, but I can breathe." Rei took a piece of material from a pocket and tied it around the druid's face.

Another quake, more forceful than the previous, shook the ground and the air around them and was followed by an earsplitting crack. The druids and casters from both sides stumbled back but didn't fall.

"We don't need to push it back—keep it paced!" Arasi shouted as the dust stung his eyes. They needed to hold on until the ground was finished tormenting itself and find an opening to move back and allow the other druids to step in.

A third tremor, greater than the first two combined, shattered the air and earth around them, sending the group to their knees. The debris swirled high enough to block out the sun, and for a moment, the world went dark.

"This can't be natural!" Binder Pollis called out from somewhere in the dust. "We need the other waves now or we'll be swallowed." Each step she took cracked the ground beneath them; nothing was solid.

Rei felt the emptiness beneath them too, but before he could say a word, Arasi cast another flare to the sky, pulling in the other waves.

"It really is all or nothing!" the druid shouted. "We need everyone!"

*
**

On the western side, the druids and casters held the same position, but something was off. The quake that had struck third on their side continued to grow and melt the ground away with it, far outside the transcoloration.

Rushing forward, Cadence and her troops reached the casters in time to pull them out of the chasm forming under their feet.

Binder Rina, the druid who had been leading them, yelled for them to fall back and conjured a wall of energy to stop them from moving forward. "The rumbling isn't stopping! It's growing beneath us! Continue to push but move back! Quick!" she ordered.

Cadence instructed her people to move back as well, just as the ground in front of them swiftly crumbled before their eyes. Around them, the druids and casters fought to keep the ground intact, at least long enough to reach a safe distance, but the earth was faster than they were. They found themselves running on ground that was melting away with each step.

"Urie!" Cadence yelled, and immediately, he was at her side. "The ropes"—she quickly explained—"cast them to the others while we secure them. Loop them, tie them, and wrap them around their waists with whatever spell you need to." The caster nodded; it was an easy trick done hundreds of times. It would hurt, but broken ribs or ankles were survivable. Cadence rushed along the line of troops secured to the guideline and handed them the ends of the ropes. "Secure them and hold them! Don't let go at any cost! We are not losing anyone like this!"

With seconds to spare, the lines went taut as more of the ground vanished. Urie and the few casters beside him supplemented the brute strength of the soldiers with their magic, bolstering the ropes and pulling back on the line. Startled cries and curses of pain echoed, but no one was lost. The ground in front of them and behind them had given away, but the majority of the guideline posts had stayed firm, providing them a narrow strip of sturdy land.

Guarding each movement, Cadence stood and tested the ground. The shaking had stopped, but steam still rose up around them, making it difficult to see if they were five feet up or fifty. "Let's gather everyone up on what we hope is solid land," she instructed their troops. "Urie, I hate putting all this on you, but please assist." She paused and smirked at him. "Though, you did bemoan wanting to have a great purpose earlier."

He let out a heavy sigh and shook his head. "Me and my big mouth."

Cadence tentatively surveyed the area and was thrilled to see they hadn't been stranded on a precipice after all. There was still a strip of land, only a few feet long and wide, that appeared sturdy enough for them to cross and reach solid ground. Solid, at least for now.

"Let's not waste time healing the wounded on the spot," she told Urie and the others. "As soon as someone is pulled up, escort them across, and neither of you come back. We need to get away from here. It's not stable, and this is not over yet." With care, she moved to the edge and knelt, helping pull everyone up from over the side.

*
**

Arasi and the others on the eastern side sensed the sudden ebb in energy but couldn't see through the thick dust in front of them.

"Something's not right!" Rei yelled.

"They aren't gone"—Arasi concentrated—"but they aren't able to continue. We can't think about what happened. Keep pushing back!"

The magic users worked harder to counter the rising water that began filling in where the earth had been.

A strong gust cleared the air around them, and the churning landscape began to ease. "Don't be caught off guard! Only this area is calming—hold fast to the others!" Arasi instructed. He knew they were all tired and in desperate need of reviving their energies, but it wasn't safe to be complacent.

In the distance, they heard cracking and the sound of rushing water, but they couldn't tell if it was coming toward them or away. The ground vibrated with a steady, frightening rhythm that didn't seem natural. The energy from the druids and casters across the fault was sporadic but strong enough to put Rei at ease for them. Through the dust and steam, he tried to discern where the Calon base camp had been, but nothing was visible—even the land it had been on was gone.

"Arasi!" Rei yelled, and pointed to where the base had been.

"The fault line splintered!" The druid swore. He wiped the dirt from his eyes and shook his head at Rei. "No one is dead, they're down. They can handle the fallen. Don't intervene!" Rei stared at Arasi with a pained expression and was about to say something he wouldn't agree with, before a loud crack in the distance knocked them both off their feet. "That didn't sound right!" Arasi yelled, and turned to peer farther below.

"Does any of this?" Rei yelled back, turning over and gathering his senses.

"No, but…" Arasi inched closer on his hands and knees to the edge. Rei felt the druid building up his energy. "Something is down there." His voice was difficult to hear over the rumbling earth and water. "I caught a glimpse of metal."

"Metal? We can't see anything!" Rei yelled. "Only moving rocks and mud! It's only a trick of the light on the waters!"

Arasi shook his head and crept farther to the edge. "No. I can sense it as well. Do you not?" There had been a flash of something moving with intent, not tossing with the disintegrating landscape.

Rei knew Arasi was focusing his energies on something other than the earth around them, no longer fighting with them. "Arasi, move back from the ledge. This isn't the time to be distracted. We'll leave it for later." Rei fought for his balance as another tremor coursed beneath their feet, and suddenly Arasi was nowhere to be seen.

*
**

Binder Ki-Avia was the last druid to be pulled up on the western side. She was in pain and still somewhat in shock, but she refused to follow the Regiment guard across to stable land. She grasped Cadence's arm. "Below," she wheezed, clutching her sides where the rope had swaddled her, "someone, below, still. They fell after we did, seemed to land on a flat spot. With their robes, it looks to be Binder Arasi."

Cadence stared down, stunned for a moment. "Urie, get her over to the others and—"

"No!" The caster stopped her. "The soldiers will see her over." He turned to Ki-Avia and bowed his head. "Binder Ki-Avia, please heal and see to the others. Binder Arasi is my master. I will see to him." He turned back to Cadence, and they both leaned over the side as safely as possible. Pockets of steam and dust scattered below, and they could see the quakes had left a crevice that seemed dozens of feet wide. How deep was impossible to grasp; dark, rust-color water angrily churned below, and on a ledge only inches above was the limp form of a druid in Arasi's robes. "It is Arasi. I can sense his energy. He's still alive."

"I knew something like this would happen. He never takes safety measures to heart." Cadence scrambled to her feet. "We can untie the rope from the guideposts; the length should be enough to reach him. We have to be quick."

Urie aided her. "You lower me down, bring him back up. Just don't leave me."

"Never," she promised. Without warning, another crack broke the silence, and the ground beneath them trembled. There would be no time to cross over to safety, and neither wanted to abandon Arasi. "Hang on to the rope!" Cadence yelled as they entwined it around their hands just before the ground crumbled beneath them.

For a moment, Cadence only saw a thick gray wall of dust. In the distance, she heard muffled yelling. The rope, still attached to the guideposts, had softened their fall somewhat, before collapsing with them. At first, she was unable to move, but the earth shifting once more freed her from the rocks covering them. Despite the trembling ground, she managed to sit up and shake the dirt from her eyes and ears. Blood coated the inside of her mouth, and the wetness from it oozed from other places on her body, but nothing to indicate she was anything more than banged up. Beside her, Urie groaned and coughed. "I think I am alive. Are you?"

"I am. I think." He shook his head. Aside from obvious scratches, he appeared unharmed; Cadence had borne the brunt of their fall.

"You had to say we'd end up as earth food, didn't you?"

"You thought I was being funny, but I was predicting the future."

"What now, then, gifted seer?"

Urie hacked the dust from his lungs. They were on a ledge a few feet wide, and rising up below them through the steam was water. "Fish food?" Suddenly, he jumped up. "Arasi!" The quake had thrown them down only a few feet from the ledge where the druid's body was. If the ground had been more stable, and his legs not weakened from the fall, Urie could have jumped across. Instead, he lowered himself and crawled toward the edge.

"Is he still alive?" Cadence asked, too concerned about their situation to be distressed.

Urie nodded. "He is, but unconscious. Likely exerted himself trying to break his fall and not land in the rushing water. The ground must have swallowed him. But, then, how did he end up over here?"

"Rei?" She tried to peer up to the other side of the crevice but couldn't see anything. Cadence's skin turned icy as she thought the worst.

Urie scanned the ridge as well. "I can sense that everyone is above us, standing back. The ground didn't collapse for them the same as it did for us, but it is as unsteady as sand. I can tell if Rei is not near, but he's there. Somewhere. He may be unconscious too, but alive."

A relieved sigh escaped her chest, and Cadence nodded. "I'm going to believe that you are right and we really have no casualties. We have to hurry and find a route out of here though or we'll be guaranteed to be among them."

Binder Rina and the others peered over the edge above, having taken a few moments to heal. "Hold tight!" she called down to them, her voice sounding miles away. "We're gathering the rope from the fallen guidelines. We'll get it down to you in a moment. Try not to move!"

"Easy for her to say." Cadence grimaced. "We're not the ones doing the moving."

Urie shook his head at her. "Even if the rope reaches us, the chance of all of us getting pulled up, without causing anyone else to tumble over, is scant. We haven't got much time, and I can tell how weakened the druids and casters are." Urie knew that they were concentrating on holding the waters back, but their energy wasn't going to last much longer. "If even one of them stops focusing on the waters, it might swell up and take us in a heartbeat." Urie stared up at them and recognized their pained expressions. "They're already exhausted. They won't be able to save all of us and hold their positions, and my abilities aren't much help from this angle."

Cadence was tentatively hopeful as she took stock of what was around them, but there was little that proved helpful. "Any climbing or levitation spells?" she asked the caster.

Urie promptly studied the distance and frowned. "Levitation requires a massive amount of energy that I don't even have on a well-rested, non-world-shaking day. We could try to etch steps, but the earth isn't solid enough—"

Just then, a loud crack echoed from all sides, and another violent tremor shook. The ledge began to crumble away beneath their feet.

"Grab on to anything you can!" Urie shouted. Steam and spray from the encroaching waters surrounded them as a hailstorm of rocks and debris came rushing as they began to fall. "Arasi!" With his last bit of energy, Urie lunged forward.

Chapter Eighteen

Cadence grabbed for Urie's waist as the ground sank beneath them. As they began to plummet, she closed her eyes tightly, desperately thinking how best to break their fall, blindly reaching with her free hand to get a hold of anything to stop them. She expected that they wouldn't make it; the rushing waters would drown them if they weren't crushed first, but she didn't want to succumb to those thoughts yet.

The shouting of the magic users above them grew fainter, but Cadence didn't know if it was from the growing distance or the earth clogging her ears. Or was it water now?

Pain suddenly shot through her shoulder as her body connected with something solid and stopped falling. She wasn't sure if she had cried out or not, but there was now grit adding to the blood in her mouth. Panic gripped her as her arm released from Urie, but she had no control over her body to hold further.

For a few seconds, everything went black, and it took Cadence a moment to regain her thoughts and movement. Slowly, she realized everything around them was eerily quiet except for the coughing and breathing of someone nearby and a soft, not unpleasant humming.

Her eyes and lungs burned from the dust as Cadence rolled over onto her side and pushed herself up, her body in agony. Slowly, she realized that the ground under her was firm and that the hail of debris had stopped, the sound of rushing water was gone, as well as everything else.

Despite the pain, Cadence vigorously shook her head, clearing her nose and ears, then knelt back straining to make out what was happening around her. She was relieved to see Arasi lying a few yards away, covered in dust and battered from the fall, but undoubtedly breathing.

"Cadence," Urie whispered. She turned to see him sitting beside her, frozen. Still guarded and moving carefully, she followed his gaze and gasped. Rei was there, on his knees not far in front of them, his palms outstretched and head down in concentration. "I think he is doing this."

"Doing what?"

Urie glanced back at her and then raised his eyes above them. "This."

Cadence gazed up and around to a dizzying sight of rocks swirling above in eerie silence. Overhead, a sheath of energy arced as though they were under a dome. The humming in her ears was emanating from it. She stretched a hand upward and watched the hairs on her arm stand up. It was the same energy as that night in the garden.

Outside of the protective energy shielding them, she could make out the edges of the crevice on either side of them; everything appeared still, suspended.

Dazed from the fall, Cadence hadn't realized what broke their descent and only now became aware of the bridge under them, formed from the crumbling rocks and roots. Beneath them, the water had stopped rising and now moved like a swift river, flowing under the mass of land they were on.

"It is Rei." She nodded to Urie. "But…" Something was wrong. "Rei?" she called, but he didn't acknowledge her, didn't move. "Rei!" He remained motionless.

Forcing herself to her feet, Cadence raced to where Rei was kneeling. She called his name again, but trancelike, he didn't move. His eyes only slightly opened, his breath indiscernible, the only proof of life was the energy exuding from him. Covered in dust from the crumbling, he might easily have been a statue. Cadence gasped as blood dripped from his nose.

Cadence fell to her knees and touched his burning face. "Rei?" The energy above them sizzled, and the blood flowed faster, covering the front of his coat in crimson streaks. "Rei, you need to wake up and stop this spell," she urged.

"How did he get here so fast?" Urie knelt beside his adjunct brother, staring. "Even casting swiftness wouldn't have moved him so fast." He winced as he saw the blood dripping from Rei's face. Urie tore a piece of his robes and gave the fabric to Cadence to help staunch the bleeding.

"What spell is he casting? Can you stop it? I'd rather plummet than see him like this."

Urie was mesmerized by the energy swirling above when he, too, beheld the solid bridge beneath them for the first time. "This isn't caster magic." He struggled to his feet, stunned, and reached a hand out to the shield above them. "It's elemental. Cosmic, I'd say. Arasi couldn't accomplish this." Translucent swirls of violet and ebony shrouded them like a twilight sky. Urie bent down and touched Rei's head gently and smiled. "Impressive, but I'm not surprised." His eyes widened. "His skin is on fire." He looked at Cadence with great concern. "He needs to wake up now. If he's not accustomed to using this level of power, he's going to exert himself to death, and Arasi isn't awake to help."

Careful not to do further harm, Cadence lifted Rei's stiff head and shook him. "We're safe!" Cadence yelled. "Wake up, Rei!" A bolt of panic ran through Cadence as she held him to her. He had done the stupid thing that Arasi hadn't wanted—he should have stayed where he was. She put her arms around his waist, supporting Rei. His blood dripped onto her shoulder and down the back of her coat. "We're okay, we are all okay. Arasi, Urie, me. The quakes have stopped, Rei. It's over. Over." Her voice rang out, echoing off the makeshift dome. "Please hear me. Please stop. Rei, wake up. Quit being so difficult! Wake up!"

Rei couldn't hear her at first; she was a hint of wind a thousand miles away, but her warmth was present around him. He knew Cadence was close, but all he could see were flickering beams of light, and all he could taste was the bitterness of his own blood tickling the back of his throat. Every muscle in his body felt like stone, unmovable and cold, and yet he felt himself trembling. He desperately needed to cough, but his lungs wouldn't react.

This is cruel, Rei thought to himself, and a voice somewhere asked him how so?

"It is no crueler than your own actions to yourself," the voice said matter-of-factly.

"If I move, the collapse continues. If I remain, it will be stable."

"Is that what you want?"

"Of course not." Rei still didn't know if he was speaking out loud. The pain was growing alongside the trembling.

"Then, do as you want. If you want to move, stop restraining yourself."

"Please help me!"

Silence was the only reply, and he sensed from somewhere what felt like the sigh of a disappointed parent. "You may ask nicely of us, but why not ask nicely of yourself?"

"Why do I need to ask myself?" Rei questioned.

"Precisely. Stop questioning. Your lack of acceptance of everything has been frustrating," the voice responded, though Rei sensed it was a different speaker from the other. "You are making strides, though you did need a push."

"We pushed too hard." Yet another voice, more melodic but still disappointed, chimed in.

"Children need pushing," the first voice stated.

"I am not a child, and would you mind telling me just who you are?" Rei demanded. His head felt like it was caught in a vise, but his thoughts were gaining clarity.

The brightness around him shifted to a warmer tone, but not enough to allow his eyes to focus. There was still no response to his question, however, and Rei was acutely aware of how much time was passing. "Fine. Can you at least help stop this?"

"Stop what?" a fourth voice echoed, and Rei internally groaned. How many somethings were in this unseen audience? "As far as we can descry, you've no need of our help."

"Obviously, as none of this has been helpful." The coldness in his body began to wane as a prickling sensation engulfed him entirely. "Can I go now?" he thought, to something, but then paused and rephrased his words. "I am going now," he said to something, somewhere. "Cadence is worried."

"You have always been free to go," a voice said.

Rei shivered as the sensation of movement returned, but along with it, excruciating pain. The warmth of Cadence's arms enveloped him, and he relaxed into her.

Cadence began to sob as his arms closed around her, and she felt him take a deep breath.

Rei lifted his bloodied face, and his eyes fluttered open. "Cadence? Arasi will be mad that you went after him." His voice sounded as though he were talking in his sleep. "He never had the talk with you about risking your life—he should have." Rei gave a slight smile before his eyes rolled back and he collapsed in her arms.

In an instant, the swirls above them gave way to a glorious twilight sky as the remaining pebbles and debris fell to the ground and into the water below. As quickly as it had arrived, the energy around them came to a peaceful stop.

With Rei out of harm's way, Urie studied their surroundings. It was as though they had been picked up and dropped in a land they had never been in before; nothing around them was recognizable. A river, wide as Arasi's keep, flowed under them, with no beginning or end in sight. Had Mora truly been split in half?

"Not sure which side we're closest to. Maybe eastern? I have no energy to cast anything. I'll drag Arasi if you carry Rei," Urie offered.

The bridge Rei had created was concave, and while not steep, the climb was daunting after what they had experienced.

"I don't think either of us is in the condition to carry, drag, or even roll anyone." Cadence groaned. She sat back with Rei's head in her lap, stroking his hair. She was relieved that his skin was already starting to cool down and his breathing was steady. "I can't even walk. I think it will be understandable if we take a few minutes and wait for help."

Urie twisted over and patted Arasi's shoulder. "Master? Are you alive?"

Given no response, he lifted one of Arasi's eyelids. The druid's arm shot up and smacked his hand. "No!" Arasi grumbled, and rolled over onto the hard dirt.

Urie shrugged and lay back on the ground beside him. "I changed my mind again." Urie grinned up at the sky. "We survived. The world appears to be more or less fine. It was exhilarating. Maybe I would like more adventures."

Cadence stared into the distance, watching a line of lanterns coming toward them. "I promise you, Urie, you can have them all. I am done with this."

Chapter Nineteen

Inside the medical tent, Arasi wiped ointment onto the side of Rei's neck and placed a heavy cloth over it. Rei was breathing normally, but he hadn't woken up since he had collapsed the day before.

"Are you certain he'll recover?" It was the hundredth time Cadence had asked in the last two days.

"Still," Arasi patiently told her. "He's breathing normally, his skin is tawny instead of crimson, and he's restless in his sleep. He'll wake once his energy replenishes. Then he will require some strict rest for a few weeks." The druid pouted up at her. "Did you ask once if I was going to be okay?"

"Yes, but you were unconscious and didn't hear me. I asked dozens of times. Urie became so annoyed he almost jumped into the water."

"I'm certain that is what happened."

Cadence rubbed her tired eyes. "All you need is a drink of water and a solid nap and you're revitalized. I've also seen you fall into larger scrapes than this in the past. What did I have to worry about?"

"That's not the point." He tossed the tub of ointment to her and beckoned her to sit with him.

Cadence stared at her wise druid friend, her eyes curious. "Were you aware of how impressive Rei's binding would be?"

Arasi shrugged. "We were aware he had the potential. Though, to be honest, how powerful is shocking. I'm jealous." He leaned forward and stroked Rei's hair adoringly.

"Druids absorb their powers from an element, for lack of a better term," Arasi began. "You're aware of the debate on whether you are born with binding or develop binding as if chosen by your element itself. Nature and elemental are the norm and then the less common paths, considered environmental. Binding weather. Restoration, such as mine. Even the binding of disintegration or decay. There is no exhaustive catalog of what a druid can be capable of binding. Or being bound to, as some might say."

Arasi lost himself in thought for a moment and then continued. "Now, cosmic, such as your lover here, is quite unique and frighteningly strong. It's probably best that Rei's acceptance was late and he was able to cultivate a calm personality before experiencing the full effect. Power such as that, well, it needs a responsible owner."

"You said cosmic," Urie piped up, "but it was still daylight when this happened." He had been at Rei's side almost as much as Cadence.

"If you're going to move up to Rei's position, you're going to need to pay better attention to the studies you slept through at the Academy."

Arasi shook his head. "Cosmic is all the sky above us, the planets, the stars, the luminescence."

"Which we see at night." Urie shrugged, and Cadence put her head in her hands.

"Which is the strongest star?" the druid asked.

"This one I know!" Urie grinned. "The sun!" He paused then. "Which is during the day. I was a bit slow on that one. Let's not share that detail."

Cadence laughed. "We will." She thought for a moment. "It wasn't only the sun, but all of the stars. They are still present during the daylight—we don't usually notice them with the closest of the bunch blocking them out. At night, there are so many thousands we can look up to see unobscured. Maybe Urie is partly correct. Maybe at night, it's stronger. Night is where Rei has always been most comfortable."

"Once he is up and about, and healthy, we'll find out." Arasi acknowledged she was on the right path.

Urie peered down at his sleeping friend. "He won't be able to deny that power now. Should be an interesting surprise when he wakes up."

"No." Cadence shook her head. "No surprise. Rei has been aware all along."

Arasi agreed. "He didn't want to accept it. Accepting it makes it real, to himself and to others. This was a situation that left him little choice though. Continuing to hide it would have meant sacrificing everything. I doubt Rei realized the impact of what he was doing at the time."

"I feel terrible for him." Urie sighed, standing up to retrieve fresh supplies. "Yet also, envious. What now?"

"He needs to decide what happens next." Arasi stared at Cadence as he spoke. "He won't be able to be left alone now—people will seek him out. Best to control it on his own terms, for the purpose he chooses."

"Which is all he ever wanted," Cadence said. "Urie, would you kindly bring some water back with you?"

Arasi sat back in the chair, putting his arm around Cadence. "We have a lot of work to be done now, but paramount is Rei's recovery. He's going to have a lot of tasks when he's better." He tapped her knee. "There is a place in far north Sentan with renowned healing springs, the loveliest blossoming trees, and near absolute seclusion. An absolutely dreadful trek to make but delightfully worth it. Oh! Also, the tastiest pastries and cakes. I'll have directions drafted for you. When Rei can travel, tell him to bring you there. Have your wedding and stay a while."

"Arasi, please—"

"Don't play coy, Cadence," the druid admonished.

"I'm not. This is hurtful. You're familiar with how the council controls—"

"The council can get stuffed!" Arasi snipped. "Everyone else in Calon stayed within the safety of their borders while you were tasked with gathering and implementing the course of action. Then ended up saving more lives than any of them combined. I think you have above and beyond earned this retirement."

"Retirement?" She balked.

"You have been dutiful to Calon since your pretentious sadist Emperor Kaden bound you to service." Cadence winced. His words weren't untrue, but the man had still been her grandfather. "Thirty years on this path now, dear friend. It led us to meet and share some amazing adventures, but taking on something like this…" He let his words hang for a moment. "Like Rei, you deserve to be in control of your own terms and purposes, and I know you are tired. I witness it every time you prepare to leave when you visit us."

"The emperor, the council, they perceive it differently. Sentans care more about their people than their duty—"

"Because our people *are* our duty," Arasi interrupted. "I wish Calon would consider the same. If need be, Emperor Ki-tae himself would deliver your abdication to the council, and they won't say a word against it." He sank into the cushions and grinned. "Besides, child, I am well aware Jiyan pulled you aside to inquire about your motives, because he spoke to me first." Cadence sighed in annoyance; it further proved her actions were never hers alone. "Besides, isn't this easier than disappearing?" He smirked.

Cadence's eyes grew large. "Is nothing private? Isn't it considered bad form to use your power for spying?"

Arasi shook his head. "I am not spying. I am being observant. I am not blind to what goes on within my walls. Tsk, tsk." He winked at her, and she shook her head. "I know you were waiting for this event to pass and then disappear. Rei would have followed, whether you asked him to or not. As wrong as it sounds, we can't let Rei leave us. He's needed, and he needs us. What I told Urie is true, people will seek Rei out now. And, with that hair, there is no disappearing. What would be best is if he stayed by his own volition and not guilt nor duty, because it would satisfy his happiness. And yours to be beside him."

"It doesn't sound much like you're letting him make his own choice." Cadence turned her gaze away from him and down at Rei. For a moment, she thought perhaps they shouldn't be having this conversation so near to him. "Arasi, you know lovers often make plans of daydreams that will never come true. Promises made from sincere intentions but not realistic. Talk of disappearing was a daydream."

Arasi took her hands and pulled her to face him. "Once, you told me that the comfort surrounding you in Sentan frightened you. The climate, the food, the people felt more like home to you than anywhere in Calon, and you'd rather it be your home. Yet you continued to return to that hideous castle and suffer until you physically can't breathe. Then find reasons to escape back to Sentan. Why retreat back onto the battlefield?"

"Arasi, I'm not from Sentan," she pushed back. "I'll never be anything more than a visitor."

"As we once were to Mora! Those are words from an angry past. You need to discard such detritus. Find much more fun demons to listen to than the ones of self-doubt." Arasi batted her nose with a finger. "Poof! Let it go! You have found a place where you can breathe. It doesn't matter where you were planted and grew, home doesn't have to be the same field."

"Detritus?" Cadence rolled her eyes.

"You and Rei had no reason to ever cross paths. Both of you could have done as expected, accepted what was placed on you by your respective worlds. Both of you refused, and by some kind of magic perhaps, you made your own unique paths and they convened. What an impertinence to fate to divide those paths again."

Cadence had no argument against his words. "When he awakens, we will see what Rei wants."

Arasi lifted her chin and brought her eyes to meet his. "It is identical to your desires, but you constantly deny yourself. Why are you so afraid of being happy?"

"You are asking questions you already have my answers to. When I am happy, it gets taken away. If you are often unhappy, then it hurts less when it is taken from you."

Arasi nodded and shrugged. "While I understand the sentiment and where it comes from, there's no place for it anymore. Maybe a decade ago I would have allowed you to wallow in it, but not now. It is quite literally a new world for Mora now, a new landscape, and that in itself will have repercussions, good and bad. If ever there was a time to let go of the old and embrace the new, I would say this is it."

Cadence stared into the druid's golden eyes. "You flit too comfortably between a rogue and a wise man."

"Who would not want a wise rogue as their lover?" He grinned, proud at the thought.

Cadence ignored his comment and instead confronted him on another matter. "You fell trying to get a closer look at something, correct? Your notes said it was large, like a ship cutting through earth instead of water."

"My, what a swift change in the subject," Arasi quipped. "Cadence, I don't doubt my eyes or what I sensed. I'm steadfast in my certainty. However, none of that is a concern at this time. Healing, ourselves and the continent, is the only thing on the agenda."

"I understand it was decided that our leaders would wait until this destruction was well in the past before addressing anything further. My guess is that's no longer true. We have had an exhausting series of days, we don't yet know how the rest of Mora fared, and you've already sent notes to Ki-tae as well as Jiyan. You believe whatever this is, it's only the beginning."

"It wasn't an attempt at being covert," he told her.

"Not your strong suit, apparently," Cadence replied.

"We want all the details of anything we have encountered, while they are still fresh. And, yes, maybe this can't, or rather shouldn't, wait. It may not be malicious, but that doesn't mean the situation is not dangerous," Arasi explained.

Everything the druid told her made sense, as it often did. "Even if, by chance, I am not Prime Mediator or an active member of the Calon Empire, you'll keep me informed. Yes?" Arasi gave her a genuine look of hurt at the thought he would leave her out. A long moment of silence passed before Cadence spoke again. "You're leaving, aren't you? Once Rei is well and decides to stay."

"Eventually. But that was hardly an attempt at being covert, either."

"What are you doing?"

"Covertly? Private research." Arasi winked. "Officially? Resigning from service to the empire. I want to enjoy these years I have left and answer to fewer people."

She grinned. "I saw the empirical envelope in your pouch." Cadence cocked her head. "The gold gilt and crest. It isn't from Ki-tae."

Arasi shrugged. "The empress has always been exquisitely kind to me. My lady has graciously suggested the royal apartments on the bay would make for a cozy private research study for me, and the emperor wholeheartedly agreed."

"Interesting." Cadence grinned.

"Gives me time to do more, personal, research."

"Sounds… intimate."

"Well…" The druid shot her a sidelong glance, and they both started laughing. Arasi hugged Cadence tightly and then held her face in his hands. "You're going to be so happy, whether you want to accept it or not." He kissed her nose.

Chapter Twenty

Night had long since enveloped the camp by the time Rei finally opened his eyes.

Two lanterns near the tent entrance illuminated enough of the inside to see that the other mats were empty, and only he remained, along with Cadence. She was asleep on a mat next to him, her leg stretched out enough to gently touch his. He knew he had been asleep for a long time; he'd had moments of waking but hadn't had the energy to keep his eyes open until now. He'd dreamed of falling rocks and swirling stars stinging his skin.

Rei gingerly pushed himself up into a sitting position and attempted to stretch. The heaviness in his limbs had subsided, and he was able to move without much effort. Still, he yelped in pain as his body cramped at the sudden movement, startling Cadence awake in the process.

"You're awake." She sat up. "Are you okay?" Rei nodded but found his throat too dry to speak properly. Cadence reached for the pitcher of water next to them. "I'm sure you swallowed a lot of dirt. You'll be tasting mud for weeks," she half joked, handing him the cup.

Rei took the water from her and proceeded to cough enough to wake the entire camp. "Refreshing and deadly." His voice was gravelly. "How long have I been asleep?"

"Almost three days now," she told him. "We were getting anxious. Urie started researching necromancy spells." Cadence stood up and retrieved one of the lanterns from the doorway along with a small leather pouch from one of the tables.

"The druids have barely been able to get much nourishment into you. You must be starving." She sat back down on the mat, closer to Rei, and opened the pouch. "A small variety of nuts, seeds, and pop peas. I can also arrange honey-soaked bread strips if you give me a few minutes."

"Bird food?" He grimaced.

"Well, it is the middle of the night," Cadence told him, "Not prime mealtime. And you've been unconscious. I don't think your insides would take well to roast chicken."

"True. Pop peas, then, please." Cadence pulled a tiny bundle out of the pouch and untied it. What amounted to two handfuls of light-green peas rolled about on the cloth. "Thank you, love." Rei smiled. The lack of flavor made them almost as dry as the grit the quakes had embedded in his teeth.

"How are you feeling otherwise?" Cadence asked.

Rei thought about it for a moment. Aside from the aching, nothing seemed out of place. "Fine, I think. Despite everything, I seem to be mostly unscathed." He took another sip of water and was relieved when he didn't cough again. "Are you honest that you're well? Urie? I'd ask about Arasi, but I heard him so much in my sleep that I knew he was perfectly fine."

Cadence nodded. "All okay. Considerably banged up, but the druids took care of all the superficial injuries once the action calmed down. We were all quite lucky. Shockingly, no casualties, and anything that was more serious than a broken bone was able to be healed. See?" She motioned to the empty mats in the tent. "You're the last patient."

Rei washed down the last of the pop peas with the remaining water. "Well, what can I say? I enjoy my sleep." He smiled. He reached his hand out and touched her cheek. "You stayed safe."

She took his hand in hers and nodded. "I did. You helped. But, Rei?"

Her tone shifted the slightest, and Rei knew what question was coming. "Yes?"

"I'll be kind because you just woke up, and you did save everyone's— and I do mean everyone's—lives. But what in the entire universe happened? Please don't deflect this one."

Rei shook his head. It wasn't that she may not believe him, it was that he didn't believe it himself. "I'm not certain."

He leaned back on the mat, retracing in his mind what had last happened. "We were advancing, and Arasi wasn't heeding the plan to stay back. He kept inching forward. I saw him fall, disappear from my vision, and could see the other side of the fault crumbling away. I knew if something wasn't done, then, Arasi would be the first of all of us. For the first time, I felt panic. It compelled something in me. I asked for guidance, and then I was on the bridge, with you and Urie."

"Guidance from who?" Cadence asked.

"The stars." Rei smiled, glancing up. Through the tiniest slit in the tent, he made out a shimmer in the dark sky above them.

"Of course"—she shook her head—"and they listened to you. But, Rei, something else happened. You were frozen, we couldn't reach you. That scared me more than the sundering."

"I know." He nodded, pulling her to him and resting his forehead against hers. "That was scary to me too. I was aware of what was happening around me, I heard you from a distance, but I couldn't move."

"What happened?"

"I think…" He paused and, after a moment, laughed. "I think I was being admonished."

"Admonished?" It wasn't the response that Cadence was expecting, and she had a fleeting wonder of how hard Rei's head may have been hit during the events.

Rei nodded. "I think, perhaps, by the stars?" He rubbed the back of his head. "Maybe the stars, maybe my inner voice. Either way, someone, or several someones, were trying to get a message to me."

"Oh"—Cadence kissed his nose—"definitely the stars. They must be tired of you using them to impress women and want you to do real work now."

"Impress women? Is that what you think?" Rei in turn kissed her nose and then her chin.

"Did you not do that for me? Take the stars from the sky?"

"Mmm. Does that mean you were impressed?"

"A bit." She kissed his lips with all the gentleness she could muster.

Rei leaned back and looked up once more toward the night, then back at Cadence. The glow of her face in the flickering light brought him as much peace as it did longing. "Then, I guess I should be more thankful to them and take their advice, huh?"

"It would be the right thing to do," Cadence agreed. "And just what was their advice?"

"Stop questioning myself, I think." Rei thought that may have been one part of their guidance. "But I don't think that was the end of the conversation."

"I'm certain there is more to come, then." Cadence smoothed out the mat beneath them. "Still, excellent advice in any matter. Now, get a little more rest. When Arasi comes back in the morning, he'll barrage you with questions. You might want to play unconscious for another day." She added her blanket to his as they settled back onto the mat.

Rei's sigh broke the momentary silence. "More to come," he repeated.

"Is it worry or annoyance?" Cadence reached up, brushing the hair from his forehead and back over his ears. "Either way, we'll have an interesting adventure."

Rei took her hand and pressed it to his lips and then his chest. "Will you stay with me, then? Navigate the stars with me?" Rei asked, not nervous at all anymore.

Cadence nodded and snuggled into his arms. "Thank you for asking, but I think that's where we were headed all along."

Chapter Twenty-One

Cadence woke up to what she thought was warm sunlight coming in through the windows. "Didn't we close the drapes?" She groaned and buried her face in Rei's shoulder. He turned and put his arms around her and pressed his head to hers.

"We did," he sighed, and he covered her head with the blanket before sitting up. "Must be one of Arasi's enchantments. Stay snuggled."

She happily obeyed and grimaced as he rolled over and left the bed. She was mildly content to stay beneath the somewhat dark covers until the distinct tinkling of breaking glass caused her to bolt upright.

"Rei?" She pulled the covers from her head and realized the room was somewhat dim again, but Rei was nowhere to be seen. "What did you break?"

"All is well. Now." Rei poked his head from around a corner and held up part of what appeared to be a broken glass tube of sorts. "Sunlight enchantment. It must have been left out when we were going through the other items last night. I'd forgotten that he'd used it to wake up before dawn."

"Did you… smash it?"

"Well, it doesn't stop glowing until noon, and it gets brighter and brighter." He put the broken tube into a bin with the other pieces he gingerly picked up.

Cadence sleepily cocked her head, not certain she was fully awake. "You just broke it?"

Rei climbed back into the bed and pulled half the covers to his side. He kissed Cadence's forehead and pushed her back onto her pillows. "It gets brighter *and* warmer."

"Oh, curse that, then." Cadence shook her head and snuggled back under Rei's arm.

"If Arasi hasn't missed it in all this time, he won't miss that thing now." Rei wrapped his arms around Cadence and drifted back to sleep until a more respectable time of the morning arrived.

*
**

Elsewhere in the keep, Kubo shoved the last of Urie's books onto the shelves and collapsed onto the nearby chair. "Why do you have so many books when we have a library in the keep? More than one, even." She'd spent all morning continuing to help Urie move into his new quarters and was already exhausted.

Urie gave her a withering glare. "Books are the centerpiece of any caster's home. Maybe if your intellect was indulged more, you could move up the caster ranks faster."

"Not interested just yet, thank you." Kubo gave a hearty sigh and stretched out her tired arms. "As for indulging my intellect, at least I know that stars are still around during the day." She smirked and pointed out the window toward the sun. "Besides, you can take as long as you want being the new senior. Junior is as fine a title. I can wait. You'll have the larger quarters now, isn't that terrific? It will be roomy."

Urie shrugged. "Not quite, since my family will be in here as well."

"I meant for me." Kubo grinned. "The quarters may be smaller in area, but since it will only be me, the room will be like my own kingdom." The younger adjunct looked around the room, already piled with boxes and canvas bags yet to be unpacked. As Rei's living area, everything had been meticulous and sparse; this was quite different. "Is there anything more you need help with?"

"Thank you, sister, but this is good. Lia will be here in the morning with the girls, and they can put everything where they want it."

Kubo nodded. "It will be enjoyable having them here. You have a good family—they always make me feel welcome." Urie nodded, proud at the compliment. "The atmosphere is quite different here now, with Arasi no longer master of the keep." Kubo sounded a bit melancholy. Arasi had been the only druid Kubo had served with and the only one who had acknowledged her potential. Urie understood; he'd felt very much the same.

"I don't think it will be vastly different. Well, except Rei won't snap at us as much. At least until the pressure gets to him." Urie chuckled. "Arasi resigned four months ago and he's already been back here a half dozen times. He's not too far away."

"It is comforting. We're all still family."

Urie grimaced. "I guess if you see it that way. Oh. Here." He handed Kubo a small cloth bag. "Take this to Cadence, will you? Lia used the plum wine to make soaps, and Cadence wanted to test it." He held out the bag, but Kubo shook her head.

"Um, why don't you deliver the bag? Or have Lia do it tomorrow? That might be safer?"

"And why?"

"I don't like bothering them." Kubo shrugged. "I sense I'm always interrupting something."

"Well, you probably are, to be honest, but you're going to have to get used to that." Kubo smirked. "Probably doubly used to that, since you realize, I'll have my wife here too. So…"

"I thought Arasi could be bad when the emperor was around!"

"Oh, but that was tame compared to years ago. When you've gained some worldliness, we can regale you with some great tales of debauchery!"

"No! Truly! I'm fine with what I currently know. I'll go take those to Cadence." Kubo snatched the bag and turned, running smack into Rei, who had quietly arrived at the door. "Oh! Sorry, Master Rei."

"Don't call me that…" Rei began, but Kubo quickly disappeared through the doorway. He shook his head at Urie. "Stop tormenting her. She's been practicing her tribulation spells extra diligently. Think I may have spied your name in her notes." The suppressed laughter in his tone made the admonishment pointless, and they both smiled. "Besides, things were never that interesting around here. Best part of all the rumors."

"Truth! We can't let on how mundane this place was—where is the fun in that?" Urie grinned. "Anyway, Master Rei has a nice ring to it, wouldn't you say? Or do you prefer Binder Rei? Which formality are you selecting?"

"Neither?"

"Oh! I've got it!" Urie raised a finger in thought. "Binder Ki-Rei! Master of Stars!"

"Decisively no," Rei said, leaning against the door and peering into his former apartment. "Bad enough Arasi tried to reason my name was too boring to be a druid and tack on 'Ki'- at least."

"Your name isn't boring," Urie said in agreement. "I like your name."

"Thank you, better than Urie, at least." He smirked. Rei took in the changes in his old quarters. "It looks vastly different. Mind if I come in?"

"You are seriously going to ask permission?"

"It's manners. Try them." Rei inspected the bookcases and boxes on the floor. "You need more books," he declared without the slightest hint of sarcasm. "Will this be enough space for you and the family? We can push into the additional quarters if you'd like."

"Maybe when the girls are older. Or if there are any additions. For now, no. That's generous, but we will be comfortable with this." Urie smiled. "Thank you, Rei."

"How are your new quarters?" Urie asked. "Sorting through all the leftovers from that other fellow?"

Rei nodded. "We are finding some amusing items. Master Arasi worked on so many different projects that even he forgot about some of them when we had to stop and focus on the divide."

"What are we going to focus on now?" Urie asked. "We were so needed these last few years—does it matter now?"

"One mustn't be needed to have work to do," Rei offered. "Even before all the world was churning, we were learning and discovering, cataloging and researching. Now our focus is healing, which will always be needed." Rei hadn't agreed with the decision to put off investigating the quakes, but he also didn't want to start the worrying all over again. They all needed rest, and ignorance enabled a deeper sleep.

"Our world was exciting for a while though, and I have to admit I enjoyed some of it." He offered Rei a seat.

Rei settled into the chair nearest the windows. "You got your first bite of adventure. Is that good or bad?"

"Both? I've only been a caster. You at least had military adventures."

"Adventures make it sound fun. That's not altogether accurate." Rei shook his head. "At this point, that was only a fraction of my life. I've been a caster ten times more seasons than my soldier career."

Urie nodded. "Life was different for a while, which was a welcome change of pace."

Rei stared out the window at the view that had been his for years. "Well, it's not over yet, so I wouldn't settle into tranquility if I were you. Between what initiated the quakes and what was seen at the south shore after the sundering, there are plenty of pieces to put together."

"Even so"—Rei smiled—"our world is more than only what Sentan, or even Mora, offers you. You can decide to study elsewhere. The western continents have begun opening their borders more often."

"No, not an option. That would mean leaving my family, which includes you, and honestly, Kubo. Don't tell her."

Rei understood. "Still an option though, if only short term. I don't want you to believe you're obligated to stay here."

Urie gave his friend a dubious look. "Is it that you feel obligated to say that?"

In response, Rei rolled his eyes and continued, "Cadence still has business to finish up in Calon. Lia and the girls have never traveled far, have they? With the trade routes and centers on their way back up to almost full function, the trip would be an enjoyable one. Why not accompany her? All of you?"

"It sounds like you're either trying to get rid of me or broaden my experiences." Urie smiled. "Might entertain the idea, though." The now senior-adjunct gazed out the window as well and then back at Rei. His friend had changed entirely, yet at the same time, not at all. "You're handling the druid role well, so far at least, considering you were vehemently against it."

"I was vehement, was I?" He winced as Urie nodded. "It wasn't a proper fit before. Guess more than the lands have shifted, and now, well, it appears to fit me now." Rei looked pleased with that. "I'm perfectly at peace with things not changing again anytime soon though." He laughed. "That was a lot at once!"

"It was," Urie agreed. "I had a thought or two it might go this way at some point. You moving on to druid, that is. Even you have to agree with that on some level. You were determined to avoid it, but I think you didn't grasp how well druid life fit at the time. This change wasn't unexpected to me. Wedding was a surprise though."

Rei grinned. "Absolutely not where I thought my path was leading.

Never entertained the thought of leaving this room." He sighed. "I was content to reach this place. Anything more was luck."

"Luck?" Urie shook his head. "I've put up with you well over a decade and luck isn't your thing. No. You forged a path so dedicated that only fate knew where it led. All you had to do was stay the course, and here you are. That's not luck, it's devotion. Something you are borderline obsessive about." Urie coughed. "Cadence."

Rei laughed and shrugged. "Devotion, huh? I guess that's not a bad thing." He stood and walked toward the door. "Thank you, brother."

"Oh, Rei? Make sure you and Cadence always act slightly annoyed and disheveled whenever Kubo comes to your quarters, please?"

"You know one day she's going to get wise to you."

"And then the apprentice will be ready to move up." Urie grinned. "Until then, she's fair game."

"Something tells me that the game isn't going to end in your favor one of these days." His words were in jest, but there was enough truth in them that Urie gave a nervous chuckle. "Thinking about it, I wonder if I absorbed Arasi's proficiencies while you were gifted with his witticism."

"Makes sense. He always thought I had no sense of humor. I wouldn't be surprised if it was some type of enchantment."

"No enchantments necessary." Rei smiled. "I guess we've all just changed a bit."

Urie nodded. "So, next adventure? Earthquakes and flooding done, perhaps a refreshing meteor shower? Volcanic explosions?"

Rei waved a finger at his friend. "You're going to feel terrible if you find out you were gifted Arasi's foresight ability."

"Light rain?" Urie offered.

"At worst," Rei agreed. He turned toward the door and promptly bumped into Kubo, who had just rushed into the room.

"No entering without knocking!" Urie admonished her. She glared at him and thrust an envelope, already opened, into Rei's hands.

"This arrived a few moments ago. Royal carrier and marked urgent, so I did a quick peruse." She stepped back, noticing their judgmental glares. "Anything urgent from the office of the empire applies to all of us, does it not?"

Urie shook his head and snorted at her excuse. "Weak."

Ignoring him, Kubo stared up at Rei, who was busy studying the letter. "She has a sound point." Rei shrugged, his eyes crinkling in an obvious grin as he looked over the top of the page. "But, then, the bulk of the responsibility for whatever the ask is will shift to whoever opens the letter first. No matter what the ask is." Kubo nodded eagerly, making Rei second guess his glib remark.

"From Arasi?" Urie asked. "So we have directions, I assume."

"Premonitions now?" Rei grinned.

Kubo nudged Urie's elbow. "Easy guess." She reached up, claiming the page from Rei's hands and pulled her well-worn notebook. "He lists a few things we need to bring with. I'll get started as I pack our bags."

"I'll pack my own, thank you," Urie said, waving his eager counterpart off.

"No you won't." She grinned. "It's your turn to stay behind. Tell him, Master Rei."

Rei held up his hands. "That's for the two of you to settle." He turned to walk away but spun back around. "Without magic," he added. He made it a point to look Kubo in the eyes as he said it, with only the slightest hint of a smile.

"I want to leave for the castle in the next day, so let's be quick on Arasi's requests," Rei added as he reached the doorway of the caster's quarters. "You wanted more adventure, Urie, I guess foresight it is!"

About the Author

Crystiannia Ryce scribbles stories set in fantasy worlds with a diverse array of lovingly crafted imaginary friends--a skill honed growing up surrounded by more books than people.

Tied to her New Jersey roots, Crystiannia lives on the Bayshore with her partners and offspring. When not writing, she can be found sleeping, reading, or at her desk daydreaming. Not quite the introvert she claims to be, you may also find her volunteering and supporting her community (as well as in the pit at nearby J-rock concerts).